This Book Belongs To

....

My Illustrated Classics Collection

Silver Dolphin

Silver Dolphin Books
An imprint of Printers Row Publishing Group
10350 Barnes Canyon Road, Suite 100, San Diego, CA 92121
www.silverdolphinbooks.com

All notations of errors or omissions should be addressed to Silver Dolphin Books, Editorial Department, at the above address. All other correspondence (author inquiries, permissions) concerning the content of this book should be addressed to

Hinkler Books Pty Ltd
45-55 Fairchild Street
Heatherton Victoria 3202 Australia
www.hinkler.com

Illustrators: George Ermos, Agnès Ernoult, Lee Holland, Lyn-Hui Ong, Geraldine Rodriguez, Javier Salas and Patricia MacCarthy.

Text adapted by: Katie Hewat
Design: Paul Scott and Patricia Hodges
Editorial: Emily Murray

ISBN: 978-1-6841-2149-6

Manufactured, printed, and assembled in Guangdong, China.

22 21 20 19 18 1 2 3 4 5

CONTENTS

Thousands of books are written and released every year, but only a few of those become great classics. These books are the ones that are read by each new generation and passed on from parents to children. They're studied and talked about. They stay with you after you finish them. People read them and then return to reread them over and over again.

There are lots of reasons why certain books become classics. They're so wonderfully written that they can transport you away to a different place or time. Regardless of how unfamiliar or different the setting of the book is, the characters seem real, with genuine emotions and authentic experiences. Most of all, it's perhaps the connection that the reader has with the characters that makes a book a classic.

There are lots of great reasons to read the classics of literature. As well as knowing that you're reading a great book, proven by the test of time, you're also expanding your vocabulary, improving your intellect, and learning about history and what life used to be like in different time periods and in different places. Reading a classic means you're listening directly to a voice from the past, speaking straight to you and other readers today.

Enjoy these classic tales and become part of a great tradition of reading and sharing stories that have entertained and captivated readers for generations!

PETER PAN

Based on the original story by

J.M. BARRIE

It was a quiet night at Number 14, where Wendy Darling and her younger brothers, John and Michael, were fast asleep in their cozy beds. Their mother, Mrs. Darling, was also sound asleep in a rocking chair beside the small fire. She had been reading the children a bedtime story and the book lay open across her lap.

Suddenly, there was a rustle of curtains and a quiet thud on the floor. Wendy opened her eyes, and saw a small boy sitting in front of the window, crying. She hopped out of bed and crept toward him. She saw that he wore an outfit completely made of leaves.

"Who are you?" she asked. "And why are you crying?"

The boy sniffed and wiped at a tear.

PET
ER

"I'm Peter Pan," he said. "My shadow came off, and I can't seem to put it back on. I've tried sticking it with soap and tying it with string, but nothing has worked. I can't get by without it." He held a crumpled black shape in his hands. Wendy asked if she could see it and Peter handed it over. She looked at it for a few moments, then went to a drawer and pulled out her sewing kit.

"This might hurt a little!" she said, but Peter was willing to try anything to get his shadow back. Wendy began sewing and Peter found it didn't hurt at all.

After a few minutes, Wendy looked up and said, "There! Good as new."

Peter stood and tried out his shadow. He ran around in circles and did a little dance and it followed him exactly like it should. Peter grinned from ear to ear and thanked Wendy, then realized he didn't even know her name.

"I'm Wendy," she said. Peter put on his best manners and gave a little bow.

"Most pleased to make your acquaintance," he said and Wendy giggled.

"Where are you from?" asked Wendy.

"I'm from Neverland," Peter replied. "It's the second star on the right and straight on till morning."

"Neverland!" exclaimed Wendy. "Why, I often visit Neverland in my dreams. It's a wondrous place full of fairies and mermaids and pirates. How wonderful it must be to live there."

It was then that Peter had a grand idea. "How would you like to come with me? You could be my new mother."

Wendy thought this a very odd request, as she was only a few years older than Peter. The idea of being the one in charge all the time sounded splendid though, so she agreed.

"You can fly, can't you?" asked Peter.

"Of course I can't fly!" replied Wendy.

"I can," said Peter, "and I can teach you!" With that, he leaped into the air and zoomed around the room.

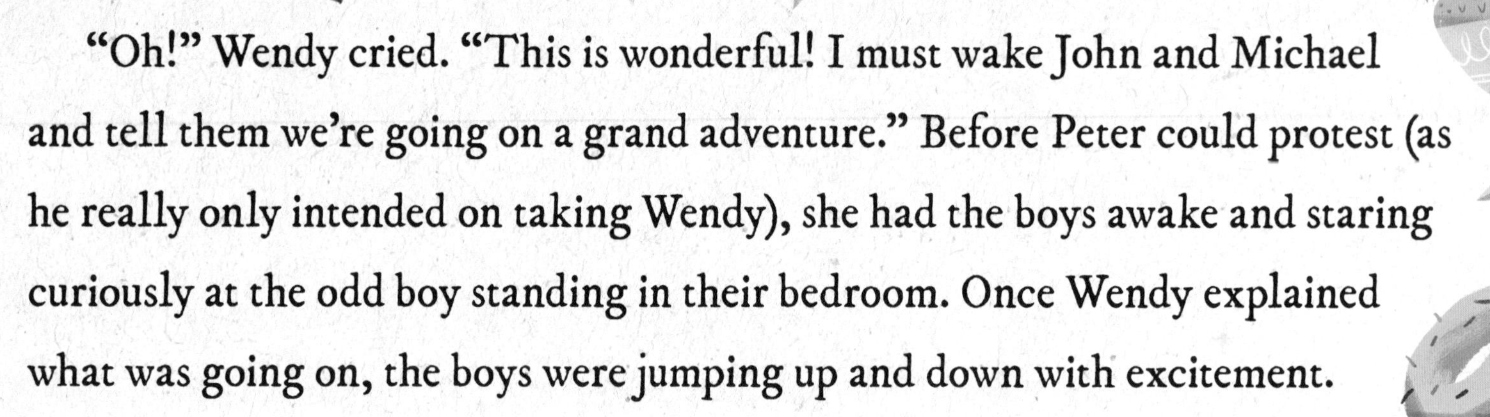

"Oh!" Wendy cried. "This is wonderful! I must wake John and Michael and tell them we're going on a grand adventure." Before Peter could protest (as he really only intended on taking Wendy), she had the boys awake and staring curiously at the odd boy standing in their bedroom. Once Wendy explained what was going on, the boys were jumping up and down with excitement.

Peter began to teach Wendy, John, and Michael how to fly. He ordered them to stand on John's bed in a line, think happy thoughts, then simply lean forward and take off.

All three children did this together. They thought of cupcakes and picnics and days by the sea, then they held hands, leaned forward and out, and...

THUMP! They all landed in a heap on the floor. John rubbed his head, Wendy rubbed her elbow, and Michael glared at Peter, believing he had been tricked. Wendy looked across at her mother, and was relieved to see she was still soundly asleep.

Peter looked sheepish. "Oops!" he said. "I forgot the main ingredient." He gave a quiet whistle and in through the window flew a tiny fairy, wearing a dress made of shiny green leaves. "This is Tinker Bell," said Peter as the fairy landed on his shoulder. Wendy smiled and said hello—she was delighted to meet her first ever fairy—but Tinker Bell just crossed her arms and harrumphed. You see, Tinker Bell was quite a jealous fairy and she was worried that Wendy might become Peter's new best friend.

"Aw, don't be like that, Tink!" said Peter.

Tinker Bell rolled her eyes. "Fine!" she grumbled, then flew across the room to the children and sprinkled a little shimmering golden dust on each of them. At once, the children felt lighter and soon they were floating around the room. It was a wonderful feeling! John picked it up easily and began doing loop-de-loops. After a little more practice, they were all flitting around effortlessly and were ready to go.

As she crouched on the windowsill, ready to leave, Wendy turned back and blew a kiss to her mother and another to her father, who was asleep downstairs. Then she launched herself out into the night and soared up into the sky.

Wendy looked down on her house, her street, and her town, thinking how very different things looked from way up there. Wendy, John, and Michael swooped down over villages and rivers, then they flew out to sea, diving down over ships and whales. They got tired at times. Young Michael kept falling asleep and tumbling to earth, but each time Peter would swoop down and catch him.

During the journey, Peter told them all about his life in Neverland. He explained that he lived with a group of friends called the Lost Boys.

"At the moment, there are seven of us," he explained, "but that changes all the time. They all stay for a while, but they leave when they grow up."

"Will you leave when you grow up, too?" asked Wendy, and Peter was horrified.

"I shall never, ever, ever grow up!" he said. At first Wendy couldn't understand what he meant, so Peter explained that he had been a boy for many, many years and he never got older.

"How many years?" asked Wendy and Peter shrugged.

"A hundred? A thousand? I'm not sure. Just forever."

"But don't you want to grow up?" asked Wendy. "Don't you want to have a job and your own house and a family?"

"I never want to have to grow up and do boring grown-up things like work every day and pay bills and complain about working and paying bills." Wendy thought about it and had to agree. "Besides, I already have my own house and the Lost Boys are my family. And now we will have a mother too."

At last Peter pointed to an island far below. "There it is," he said. "That's Neverland!"

Wendy recognized it at once. She had seen it before in her dreams.

"Look down there," said John. "There's a pirate, asleep in the grass."

"Well, at least the pirates don't seem too scary," said Wendy.

Peter scowled. “You wouldn’t say that if you met Captain Hook,” he said. “He is my sworn enemy. One day he was chasing me across the lagoon and as he reached down to grab me, a great crocodile came snapping out of the water and bit his hand right off. The crocodile found it so delicious that he’s followed Hook everywhere ever since, trying to grab another tasty bite. Now he has a hook for a hand and he blames it all on me.”

“Well, let’s hope we don’t bump into him!” said Wendy.

On the far side of Neverland, the Lost Boys were being chased by pirates. They pounded through the forest with the pirates in hot pursuit until they reached their underground home. Above the house were seven hollow trees: one for Peter and each Lost Boy. Each boy climbed into his tree and slid down into their home.

Realizing the Lost Boys had vanished, the pirates sat down to rest. Captain Hook sat on a large mushroom. "I wonder when Peter Pan will return?" he said. "I'd love to get my hook into that brat!" Suddenly, he leaped up from the mushroom. Smoke was billowing from his pants! "I'm on fire!" Hook shouted.

Hook hopped from leg to leg, patting his backside and trying to put the fire out. He spied a muddy puddle and plonked down in it. Steam and smoke hissed around him and he sighed with relief.

Now he was out of danger, Hook was most curious about the mushroom, and it didn't take long to find out that it hid a chimney to an underground house. Hearing a voice, Hook leaned down to listen. "Peter will be back tonight!" a boy said.

Captain Hook was delighted. Peter, his greatest enemy, was coming back and Hook had stumbled upon his secret home . . . not that he had found a way in yet. But his joy didn't last long, as another sound filled his ears: Tick-tock! Tick-tock! Tick-tock!

Hook went white: he knew that noise anywhere! Now, Hook was a fearsome and mostly fearless pirate, but there was one thing he was terribly afraid of. The crocodile that had swallowed his hand had also eaten a clock, and Hook could hear the clock, ticking away in its belly. The crocodile had found him!

Peter and a very grumpy Tink led Wendy, John, and Michael through forests and fields and over mountains until they reached a pretty patch of trees beside a shimmering lake.

"Home sweet home," said Peter. Wendy looked around but she couldn't see anything that looked like a house.

Peter gave a loud whistle. A few moments later, heads popped out from six of the trees. "These are my friends, the Lost Boys," said Peter. He introduced each one as they came out to meet Wendy, John, and Michael.

"This is Tootles, Nibs, Slightly, Curly, and the Twins. We can't tell the twins apart, so we don't bother calling them separate names."

"Wendy is going to be our mother," Peter told the boys, and they were overjoyed. Tinker Bell wasn't quite so pleased. When she was sure nobody else was looking, she poked her tongue out at Wendy and flew off into the forest.

"Hooray!" shouted Tootles. "You can cook for us and wash our clothes and darn our socks!"

Wendy had thought that being the mother meant that she could boss everybody around, but this was starting to sound like a lot of work.

Peter led Wendy and the boys to a tree in the center and climbed up it, gesturing for the others to follow. Once they reached the top, they slid down a chute in the trunk and landed in a spacious room. Wendy was quite surprised. It was a whole underground house! Peter showed them around, allocating each of them a bedroom. They'd never had their own rooms before!

Over the following weeks, the Darling children explored Neverland with Peter and the Lost Boys: they fished in the lake and climbed trees, played pirates and made mud pies. Wendy taught the boys how to cook the fish they caught.

One day they met a group of mermaids who lived in the lake. Wendy had been very much looking forward to meeting them, but found that mermaids weren't very friendly. They spent most of their time brushing their long silky hair and staring at their reflections in the lake. As Wendy and the boys were sunning themselves on an island in the middle of the lake, the pirates came. There were three of them: Captain Hook, Gentleman Starkey and Hook's bosun, Smee.

"Quick!" Peter said to Wendy. "Take the boys to safety. I'll take care of these pirates."

As Wendy and the boys swam across the lake to their underground home, the menacing pirates climbed out of their boat and ran at Peter, waving their swords. "I've got you now!" roared Hook.

Peter picked up two stones, took aim, and threw them. The first grazed Starkey on the side of his head and the second broke Smee's glasses. The two pirates howled and ran for the safety of the boat.

Now it was just the two archenemies, Peter and Hook, standing on the little island. They circled each other, then suddenly Peter launched himself at Hook. The pair struggled and grappled, spun and wrestled, until Peter lost his footing and crashed to the ground. Hook stood over him, a wicked grin on his face. Peter was sure that he was done for.

But then came that old familiar sound: Tick-tock! Tick-tock! "The crocodile!" Hook shrieked, and he took off toward the boat, leaped over the side, and ordered the others to row. Peter stood up, brushed himself off, and laughed, waving to the pirates as they pulled away from the island. This made Hook more furious than ever.

The next weeks passed without any sign of the pirates, and the children went back to enjoying themselves, playing games and exploring. But after a while, Michael began to ask when they could go home, as he missed their mother and father. Wendy and John also missed them, and eventually they decided it was time to leave.

When they told Peter and the Lost Boys, everyone was very sad. Peter wouldn't let his hurt feelings show, but the other boys cried and wailed and begged Wendy to stay. She was sad to leave, but it also made her sad to think how much her parents must be missing them.

Tink, on the other hand, was not sad at all, and happily volunteered to take them home. "Today, if possible," she said, "but right now would be even better!" This was the most cheerful Wendy had ever seen Tink.

When the day came for Wendy, John, and Michael to leave, the Lost Boys went to see them off, but Peter wouldn't speak and refused to get out of bed. As soon as they had left the house, he cried himself to sleep.

Outside, there were lots of tearful farewells. Wendy hugged each Lost Boy, and then hugged them again. They made her promise to come back and visit, and she said that she would. Just as Tink was about to sprinkle the children with fairy dust, there was a great roar and a group of pirates burst out from the trees, led by Captain Hook.

"Seize them!" cried Hook. The pirates rushed at the children, grabbing them and holding them still as others tied them up. They tried to catch Tinker Bell, but she was too fast and zipped off into the forest.

Hook looked around, realizing that Peter was nowhere to be seen. He was livid. When he questioned the children, they all told him Peter was gone. "I suppose you lot will have to do then," Hook said, and he marched the children off through the forest and onto his waiting ship.

Once on the ship, he gave them a choice. “Anyone who wishes to become a pirate can join my crew,” he said, “and the rest will walk the plank!” The children were very afraid of walking the plank, but anything seemed better than joining his pirate crew, so they all refused. Hook shook with rage.

Back at the underground house, Tink, who had waited in the trees until the pirates had gone, was furiously trying to wake Peter. Finally, Peter woke up, rubbing his eyes and asking what all the fuss was about. When Tink explained what had happened, Peter leaped out of bed, ready to rescue his friends.

On the ship, the furious Captain Hook was readying his first prisoner to walk the plank. Tootles was blindfolded and two burly pirates led him to a plank that stuck out from the side of the ship. But just at that moment they all heard it: the tick-tocking of the crocodile! Captain Hook began to whimper. "Hide me!" he called to his men. They ran around in circles bumping into each other, unsure of what to do. Finally, Smee opened a cupboard and pushed Hook inside.

Tootles, who was still standing on the plank, lifted his blindfold and looked down. He discovered that the tick-tock wasn't coming from a crocodile at all—it was Peter Pan swimming in the water with a clock of his own. In the midst of all the confusion, Peter snuck aboard and untied all of his friends.

By this time, all the pirates had lined up along the side of the boat and were leaning out over the water, looking for the crocodile. On Peter's word, the children rushed up behind the pirates and shoved them over the side. They landed in the water with a great splash, and had no choice but to paddle to shore. The children cheered as the pirates swam away.

"Now that they're taken care of," said Peter, "it's time to deal with Hook!" He stood outside the cupboard and called to Hook in Smee's voice, "It's safe now . . . The crocodile is gone."

When Hook opened the cupboard he was shocked to find Peter standing there. "You!" he roared.

"Yes, me!" said Peter, feeling quite proud of himself.

Peter picked up two swords from the ship's deck and passed one to Hook. "Now, let's finish this once and for all."

Hook jumped out of the cupboard, slicing his sword through the air. Peter, however, was very fast: he ducked and weaved and avoided most of the blows. Occasionally their swords met with a clang and they stepped back and swung again. Peter and Hook were evenly matched; on and on they fought, until both were exhausted.

Peter managed to push forward to corner Hook against the side of the ship. Hook was tiring faster than Peter, and he realized that he would lose if he didn't do something quickly. He jumped up onto the ship's rail, deciding that he would swim to shore and live to fight another day.

"This is not the last you'll see of me, Peter Pan!" he yelled, then jumped over the side. But on his way down, he saw with great horror that his nemesis, the crocodile, was waiting for him below. It opened its huge jaws and in Hook fell. With one great gulp, Hook was gone.

Wendy and the boys cheered Peter and he gave a little bow. They were very relieved to have rid Neverland of Captain Hook. In years to come, the Lost Boys would find that the other pirates were quite friendly fellows without the terrible captain's influence.

Once again it was time for Wendy, John, and Michael to say goodbye, but this time Peter decided to take them home himself. After more hugs and tears and a sprinkle of fairy dust, they were up and away, crossing mountains and fields and forests, flying over seas and rivers and villages, until they finally reached their own town, their own street, and could see their open bedroom window at Number 14.

They flew in the window and landed quietly. They were quite shocked to see Mrs. Darling was fast asleep by the fire, exactly where the children had last seen her. Wendy gave Peter a huge hug and thanked him for looking after them through all their adventures.

"I'll miss you all very much," said Peter. John and Michael nodded.

"Well, you may come and visit us whenever you like," said Wendy. Peter smiled, hopped onto the windowsill, gave a last little wave, and flew off into the night.

Once Peter was gone, the children flew at their mother. Michael climbed onto her knee and John and Wendy wrapped their arms around her. She woke with a fright. "Whatever is going on?" she asked.

"We're sorry we were gone for so long!" said John.

But Mrs. Darling was completely baffled. "I don't know what you mean," she said. "I was in the middle of reading you a bedtime story." She looked at the clock above the fireplace. "Oh dear, look at the time!" And she hurried them all into their beds.

"But we met mermaids!" said Wendy.

"And we were captured by pirates!" said John.

"And a crocodile ate Hook!" said Michael.

Mrs. Darling just shook her head and smiled. "What wonderful imaginations you have, my darlings. But now is the time for all little children to be fast asleep. Sweet dreams!" And she closed the window, turned off the lamp, and kissed them all goodnight.

As Wendy snuggled into her bed, it almost felt like the whole adventure could have been a dream. But then she noticed a little sprig of flowers on her pillow. They were the same as the ones growing outside Peter's underground home and she realized Peter must have left them for her. She smiled, closed her eyes, and drifted off to sleep to dream of Neverland once again.

WONDERLAND

Based on the original story by

LEWIS CARROLL

It was a very hot day and Alice and her sister were sitting by the pond in the shade of a great oak tree. They had just finished a wonderful picnic of honey cakes and lemon cakes, banana bread and fruit scones, chocolate cookies and blueberry crumpets. Alice was very full and felt very sleepy indeed.

Just then, Alice saw a White Rabbit hurrying by the hedge, wearing a waistcoat and muttering to himself.

"Oh dear! Oh dear!" said the White Rabbit. "I shall be late. Oh dear! Oh dear!"

The Rabbit took a watch from his waistcoat pocket, looked at the time, and hurried on. Alice was very curious, and got to her feet. She followed the Rabbit and was just in time to see him pop under the hedge and down a rabbit hole.

Oddly enough, Alice didn't think it at all peculiar to see a talking rabbit in a waistcoat so, without hesitation, she followed him into the hole and found herself dropping down into what seemed to be a very deep well. The sides of the well were covered with cupboards and bookshelves, maps and hanging pictures. Down, down, down she went, until suddenly her fall came to an end with a thump! She landed on a thick pile of sticks and dry leaves.

Alice watched the Rabbit vanish through a tiny door with a tiny lock. Beside the door sat a glass table with a tiny golden key on top.

She tried the key in the lock and it opened right up! Through the door, Alice saw the most spectacular garden she could ever imagine, full of flowers and fountains and wonderful creatures.

But how would she ever fit through that door? She tried squeezing through headfirst, then feetfirst, with no luck. She closed the door and locked it, feeling terribly disappointed and wishing she had eaten fewer cakes for lunch.

When Alice stood up, she was amazed to see there was now a small bottle on the glass table. The label said "Drink me!"

Alice put the key down on the table. She checked that the bottle was not marked poison (this was a lesson she had learned the previous summer after swiping a glass of what she mistakenly thought was cordial from the kitchen), then quickly gulped down some of its contents.

"What a curious feeling," said Alice. "I feel as if I've shrunk!" In fact, she had. "How nice," she thought. "Now I can get through the door and into the garden."

Then she remembered she had left the key on the table. "Oh bother!" she exclaimed. "I'm so small I can't reach the key!"

Alice tried to scramble up one of the table legs but, about halfway up, she could go no higher and slid and slipped all the way back to the bottom.

She decided to try again and this time she was determined to make it. She backed up all the way to the door to give herself a run-up. "I've got it this time!" she said, and she took off as fast as she could. When she reached the table leg, she was racing along and she took a giant leap. She was delighted as she soared through the air, until she managed to get tangled in her skirts, missed her hold on the leg, and landed on the floor in a heap.

Alice dusted herself off and gave it one more try, before she finally sat down on the floor and burst into tears.

Once she had cried herself out, Alice noticed a small cake under the table. The icing spelled "Eat me!"

"Well, it has been a while since lunch," Alice thought, and she gobbled it up. Immediately she began to grow. "Curiouser and curiouser!" she said.

Now she could reach the key, which she placed in her pocket. But, once again, she was far too big to fit through the door.

Alice opened the door and looked through into the garden, feeling very sad. Then she noticed that the bottle on the floor still had some liquid in it, so she drank it.

She waited and waited, but nothing seemed to happen. Alice burst into tears again: giant tears that just wouldn't stop. The giant tears began making puddles on the floor, and soon those puddles joined together and turned into a flood.

When she finally stopped crying and looked around, she realized that the flood of tears was carrying her through the open door. She had shrunk after all!

DRINK
ME

Once she was through the door, Alice saw that her tears had created a giant lake, and that all sorts of creatures from the garden had fallen in.

As she swam, she made friends with a mouse, a dodo, and a parrot, and together they found their way to the edge of the lake. They climbed out, exhausted and soaking wet.

"However will we get dry?" asked Alice, which set off a rather confusing argument between the other creatures.

"We must name all the kings and queens of England, from first to last then last to first!" said the mouse.

"Nonsense!" screeched the parrot. "We must do it my way, as I am the oldest." But when asked what "his way" was, he really had no idea.

Then the dodo declared, "We must have a Dodo Race! Line up behind me!" And that seemed to settle it.

After they raced for half an hour, the dodo stopped and said, "The race is over!"

"But who won the race?" asked Alice.

"We all did, because we are all dry!" replied the dodo.

Alice giggled and thought they were all quite mad. Suddenly she saw the White Rabbit dash by, so she said goodbye and ran after him.

Alice followed the Rabbit all the way to a sweet little cottage in a clearing. The Rabbit saw her and, mistaking her for his maid, shouted, “Girl, go upstairs and find my gloves! Hurry, hurry, there’s no time to lose!”

Alice, being the kind and helpful girl she was, rushed into the cottage and ran upstairs to search for the gloves. She found a pair of white gloves lying on a bedside table.

Beside them was a little bottle filled with sparkling liquid. It looked so delicious that Alice just couldn’t resist. She picked up the bottle and, completely forgetting to check the label this time, took a little sip. Before she had even put down the bottle, she was growing.

She grew and grew until she was completely squashed inside the tiny cottage, with one arm hanging out of the window and one leg stuck right up the chimney! It was most uncomfortable.

Alice heard the front door open and footsteps running up the stairs. The Rabbit burst into the room and saw Alice. Completely terrified, he turned and dashed back out, yelling for help.

Soon, Alice could hear that a group had gathered outside and were suggesting ways to remove the giant from the house.

"We could climb through the window," said one voice.

"Or go down the chimney," suggested another.

"We'll have to burn it down!" added a third voice.

Alice was horrified. She was about to scream when some small pebbles started flying in through the window. A few landed on her nose, stinging.

"Ouch!" she cried and as she did, a pebble flew straight into her mouth. Alice was surprised and delighted to find that it was a delicious cookie! She chewed it and swallowed it and she immediately began to shrink. She was tempted to snack on a few more of the tasty treats, but she was already very small.

Alice tiptoed down the stairs and tried to sneak away, but outside she found a very cranky White Rabbit along with an angry lizard and two grumpy guinea pigs waiting for her. They began to chase Alice, so she fled away into the forest.

Alice decided that it was much too risky being this small in such a strange land, so she started searching around for something to eat that might make her taller again. Soon she came across a tasty-looking mushroom. She walked around the mushroom from one side to the other. She thought about having a nibble, but her mother had always warned her that eating wild mushrooms could make very strange things happen. Finally, Alice stood on her toes and peeked over the edge.

Alice was very surprised to see a large blue caterpillar sitting on top. And the caterpillar seemed very surprised to see Alice.

"Who are you?" he asked.

"I'm not so sure anymore," replied Alice. "I knew who I was when I got up this morning, but I have changed ever so many times since then."

Alice thought the caterpillar might be able to help with her problem, so she asked if he knew any way she could grow taller. The caterpillar explained that eating one side of the mushroom would make her grow taller, while the other would make her shorter.

Alice broke a piece off each side of the mushroom. She nibbled at one piece, which made her shrink, so she quickly took little bites from the other piece until she reached her usual height.

"What a relief!" she exclaimed. "It was such a bother being so small."

The caterpillar looked at Alice disapprovingly. "Of course you'll always be unhappy if you go around changing shapes and sizes all the time."

Alice thought the caterpillar quite rude, so she turned and walked away. "Let's see how you feel when you turn into a butterfly!" she mumbled under her breath as she left.

After a while, Alice sat down against a tree trunk to rest. She was startled to hear a voice. "Hello there," it said. Alice looked up and saw a huge cat hanging from one of the tree branches, grinning.

"Why are you grinning?" asked Alice.

"Because I am a Cheshire Cat," it replied.

The cat's grin grew a little wider. Alice decided it must be friendly, so she asked, "Would you please tell me which way I ought to go from here?"

"That depends on where you want to get to," answered the Cat.

"I don't much care," said Alice.

"Then," purred the Cat, "it doesn't really matter which way you go."

Miraculously, as the Cat spoke, Alice saw its tail disappearing, followed by its body and then its face. Finally, only the grin remained. "To the right lives the Hatter," continued the Cat, "and to the left lives the March Hare."

The Cat grinned at Alice again and its body reappeared. "You can go and visit either of them if you like, but they are both mad."

"Everybody here is mad," murmured Alice. She decided to head left.

After a long walk, she came upon a small house with two chimneys shaped like a hare's ears. Outside, at a large table, sat the March Hare and a very peculiar-looking fellow wearing a large top hat. The Hare looked up and saw Alice approaching. "No room, no room!" he began shouting.

"How rude!" said Alice. "There is plenty of room." She sat down in a chair of her choosing.

"Have some wine!" said the Hatter. Alice thought this odd, since they were clearly having a tea party.

"I can't see any wine," she said.

"Oh, there isn't any; only tea," replied the Hatter.

Alice decided there was no point arguing, so instead she asked: "Do you know the time?"

"Time?" said the Hatter. "Do you know him too? I once had to sing a song about Time for the Queen of Hearts. During the first verse, she shouted, 'You're murdering Time! Off with your head!'"

"How savage!" cried Alice.

"Oh, she wants to chop everyone's heads off. You'll see," replied the Hatter as he picked up the teapot and splashed some tea on the dormouse's nose. The dormouse squealed and jumped out of the sugar bowl.

"Oh, you're awake!" said the March Hare to the dormouse. "Tell us a story!"

"OK," said the dormouse. It rubbed its nose and began: "There were once three sisters who lived in a treacle well."

"There's no such thing as a treacle well," interrupted Alice. "What nonsense!"

"If you think it's nonsense, maybe you should just be quiet!" said the Hatter.

Alice had never met anyone so rude, or quite so mad, in her life. "That was the silliest tea party I have ever been to in my life," she said to herself, and walked on.

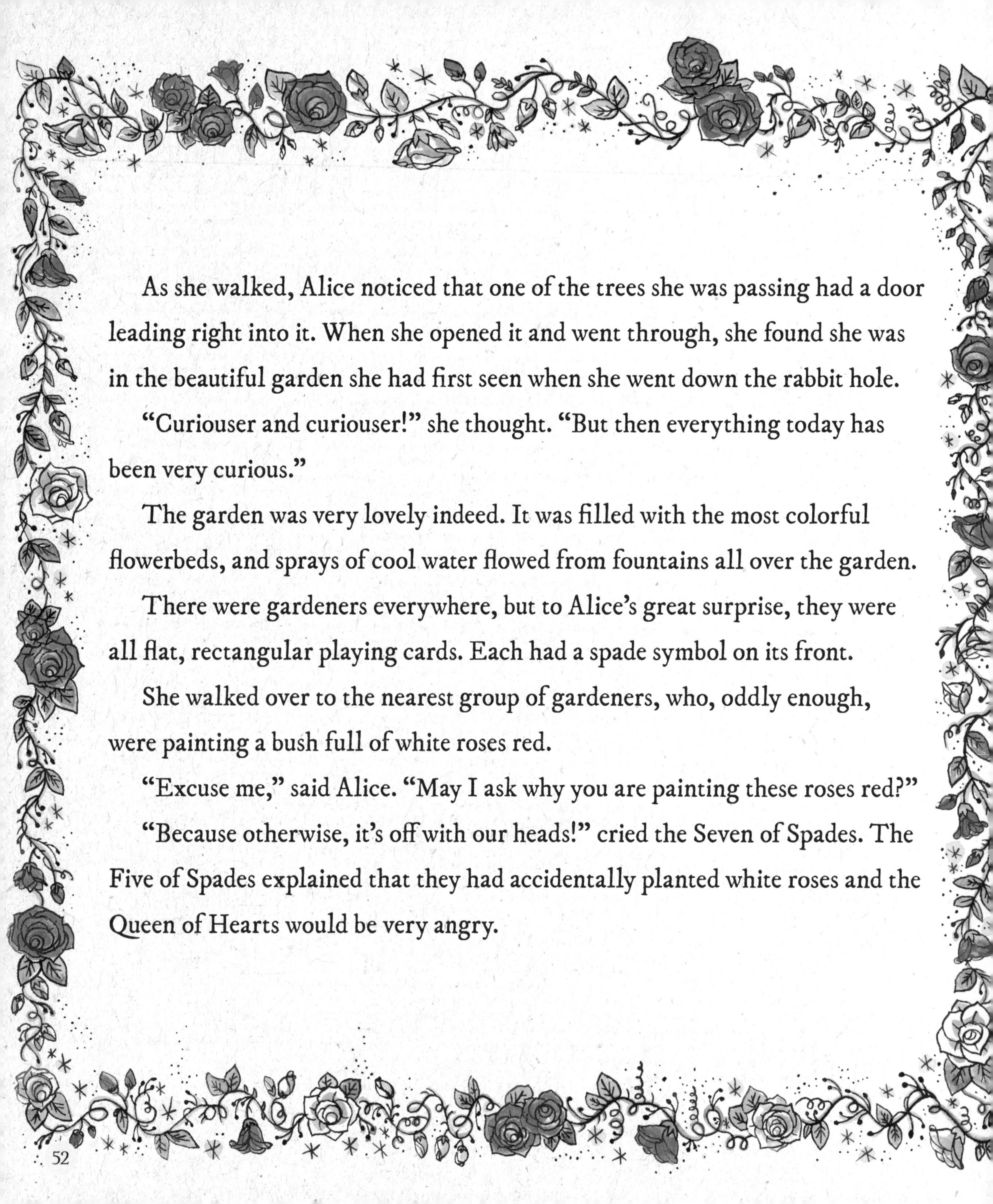

As she walked, Alice noticed that one of the trees she was passing had a door leading right into it. When she opened it and went through, she found she was in the beautiful garden she had first seen when she went down the rabbit hole.

"Curiouser and curiouser!" she thought. "But then everything today has been very curious."

The garden was very lovely indeed. It was filled with the most colorful flowerbeds, and sprays of cool water flowed from fountains all over the garden.

There were gardeners everywhere, but to Alice's great surprise, they were all flat, rectangular playing cards. Each had a spade symbol on its front.

She walked over to the nearest group of gardeners, who, oddly enough, were painting a bush full of white roses red.

"Excuse me," said Alice. "May I ask why you are painting these roses red?"

"Because otherwise, it's off with our heads!" cried the Seven of Spades. The Five of Spades explained that they had accidentally planted white roses and the Queen of Hearts would be very angry.

Just then a trumpet sounded. The Spades fell flat to the ground, shaking terribly. Alice looked up to see a procession enter the garden, led by the King and Queen of Hearts. The Queen stopped when she saw what the gardeners had been doing and flew into a rage.

"Off with their heads!" she shouted, and a group of Clubs ran forward and dragged the gardeners away.

"Wait!" cried Alice. "You can't do that!"

The Queen spun around, noticing Alice for the first time. "Nobody tells me what to do in Wonderland!" she screeched. "Off with your head!"

Just as the Clubs were about to grab hold of Alice, the King spoke quietly. "Now, now dear, let's not spoil such a lovely day. Maybe the girl could join our game of croquet?"

The Queen nodded and moved on. The King whispered in Alice's ear, "Not to worry, my dear: every time the Queen orders a beheading, I have the poor creature released as soon as they're out of sight."

He gestured for Alice to join the procession.

They soon reached a field covered with ridges and ditches and the Queen called for the game to start. It was not like any game of croquet Alice had ever seen.

The Clubs spread themselves around the field and bent over backward to form croquet hoops. The Six of Hearts handed each player a pink flamingo, which they were to hold upside-down to use as a croquet mallet. Then a group of hedgehogs waddled onto the field. One rolled up on the ground in front of each player to be used as a croquet ball!

When the game finally started, everybody played at the same time. Hedgehogs rolled into ditches and rolled up ridges to fly up in the air. Every few seconds Alice could hear the Queen shout, "Off with his head!"

Alice feared the Queen's anger, so she was doing her very best to play, but with little success. Her flamingo kept twisting its head around no matter how politely she asked it to stay stiff, which made the other flamingos panic; and the hedgehogs were getting tired of being whacked around and so were trying their best to get off the field.

The game finally ended when the King and Alice were the only remaining players whose heads the Queen had not ordered off.

Alice had just flopped down on a grassy hill, quite exhausted, when she was approached by a griffin. He was an odd creature with the wings and head of an eagle and the body and tail of a lion.

"You must come with me!" the Griffin said. "The Queen has ordered that you be taken to meet the Mock Turtle."

Alice got up and followed. "Whatever is a Mock Turtle?" she asked the Griffin, who looked at her as if she was quite peculiar.

"Why, it's what they use to make Mock Turtle soup, of course!" he replied.

Soon the pair came upon a rock, on top of which sat a curious creature who was part calf and part turtle, crying. Alice felt terrible for the poor sad creature and asked him what was wrong.

"I used to be a real turtle," he said through his sobs. "I used to swim in the ocean and go to a school. Our teacher was a wonderful old turtle we all called Tortoise."

"Why did you call him Tortoise if he was a turtle?" asked Alice.

"Because he taught us, of course!" replied the Turtle. This made Alice giggle.

"I go to school too," she said. "I take lessons in French and music and lots of other things."

"I used to take lessons in French, music, ambition, uglification, and washing clothes," the Griffin chimed in.

Alice didn't know what to say to that, so she turned back to the Mock Turtle. "How long did you spend at school?" she asked.

"Ten hours on the first day, nine on the second, and so on," he replied.

"How very odd!" said Alice.

"Well, that is the reason they're called lessons," said the Griffin. "Because they lessen by an hour each day."

Alice was still laughing at this when she heard the White Rabbit's voice carry across the meadow: "Hear ye! Hear ye! The trial is about to begin!"

"Come on!" cried the Griffin, and he took Alice by the hand and hurried off.

The Griffin dragged Alice along to the courthouse, where the King and Queen of Hearts sat on their thrones on a raised platform. The courtroom was full of every creature imaginable—in fact, it seemed like the whole of Wonderland was present.

The jury was made up of twelve creatures, a few of whom were familiar to Alice, including the angry lizard and the two grumpy guinea pigs from the Rabbit's cottage.

In the center of the room was a table upon which sat many jam tarts.

They smelled delicious. Alice was wondering if it would be rude to take a tart when the doors burst open and two Clubs dragged in the Knave of Hearts.

"White Rabbit, read the charges," said the King. The White Rabbit unrolled a scroll, cleared his throat and began:

"The Queen of Hearts, she made some tarts,
All on a summer day.
The Knave of Hearts, he stole those tarts,
And took them quite away."

The crowd gasped. This was indeed a serious charge!

Soon Alice found herself in the midst of a very bizarre trial. The Queen demanded that the jury begin the trial by deciding whether the Knave was guilty, but the Rabbit insisted on hearing from the witnesses first.

He called the first witness: the Hatter. "Well," the Hatter began, waving his teacup as he spoke, "The March Hare was..."

"No I wasn't!" shouted the March Hare, leaping out of his seat before the Hatter could finish his sentence.

"Off with their heads!" shouted the Queen, and both the Hatter and the Hare were dragged away. "Call the next witness!"

Alice was shocked when the White Rabbit turned to her and said, "We call the girl."

"What do you know of this crime?" asked the King.

"Why, nothing at all," replied Alice.

"Liar!" shouted the Queen. "Off with her head!"

Alice found herself growing quite angry. She'd had enough of this horrible queen. "I'm not afraid of you!" she shouted. "You're not even a real queen. You're all just a bunch of playing cards!"

As soon as those words left her lips, the Queen, the King, and the guards all turned into normal playing cards. They flew into the air, fluttering all over the place. Alice put her hands above her head to protect herself and gave a little scream as the cards tumbled down . . .

“Wake up! Wake up . . . ” Alice heard a faint voice saying. She opened her eyes and saw some leaves fluttering down around her. She was back under the oak tree beside the pond.

“What a long sleep you’ve had,” said Alice’s sister, who was sitting beside her.

Alice sat up and looked around, feeling very confused and a little hungry. “I’ve had the most curious dream . . . ” she said.

Based on the original story by

ROBERT LOUIS STEVENSON

I'll never forget the night I first met the bloodthirsty pirate, Billy Bones. A great storm was blowing in from the sea and the wind was shaking the walls of the Admiral Benbow Inn, which my mother and I owned and ran. Thunder bellowed and lightning streaked the sky.

Then, between the rolls of thunder, I heard a man coming down the path singing an old pirate shanty:

"Fifteen men on a dead man's chest,

Yo-ho-ho and a bottle of rum!"

This was followed by a loud banging at the door, and I opened it to find that our visitor was a tall man with a vivid red scar across his left cheek. He wore a filthy blue coat and carried a cutlass, knife, and pistol in his belt. He was dragging a heavy chest behind him, which he dropped on the floor as he entered the inn.

"I'm Billy Bones," he declared grandly. "No doubt you've heard of me?" I shook my head and he looked rather offended. "Who are you, then?" he asked.

"Jim Hawkins," I answered nervously.

"Well, Master Hawkins, do you get many visitors here?" he asked. When I told him that our inn was a quiet place, he seemed very pleased.

"Good!" he said. "I'm not wanting to see any strangers . . . or old friends for that matter," he added darkly. I served him a quick meal and showed him to his room. He lugged his trunk up the stairs and slid it under the bed.

I locked up the inn and went to my own bed, hoping that Billy Bones would not stay for long.

But Billy stayed for a few weeks, and then a few weeks more. He was a terribly unpleasant guest and he drove our other customers away. Worst of all, he constantly carried his knife and his pistol. My mother was too afraid to ask him to leave, though he had not paid her a penny since he'd arrived.

One day, another man came looking for Billy Bones. This man had a patch over one eye, two missing fingers, and a cutlass: he couldn't have looked more like a pirate if he'd bought a costume. Billy was out, so the man sat near the fire and waited. When Billy finally came back through the door, he let out a low hiss. "Black Dog, you lily-livered scoundrel!" he snarled.

"If it isn't my old friend Billy Bones!" sneered Black Dog. "I believe you have something that belongs to me and the crew."

"You'll never get that map from me," said Billy. With that, he launched himself across the room at Black Dog and a great struggle ensued. The two pirates kicked and hit and bit each other. They pulled at each other's hair and poked at each other's eyes—it was not at all like the valiant fights I had read about in my favorite pirate stories! Finally, Black Dog backed away.

"You turn over that map by ten o'clock tonight, or I'll be back with the rest of the crew!" he shouted as he ran out of the inn.

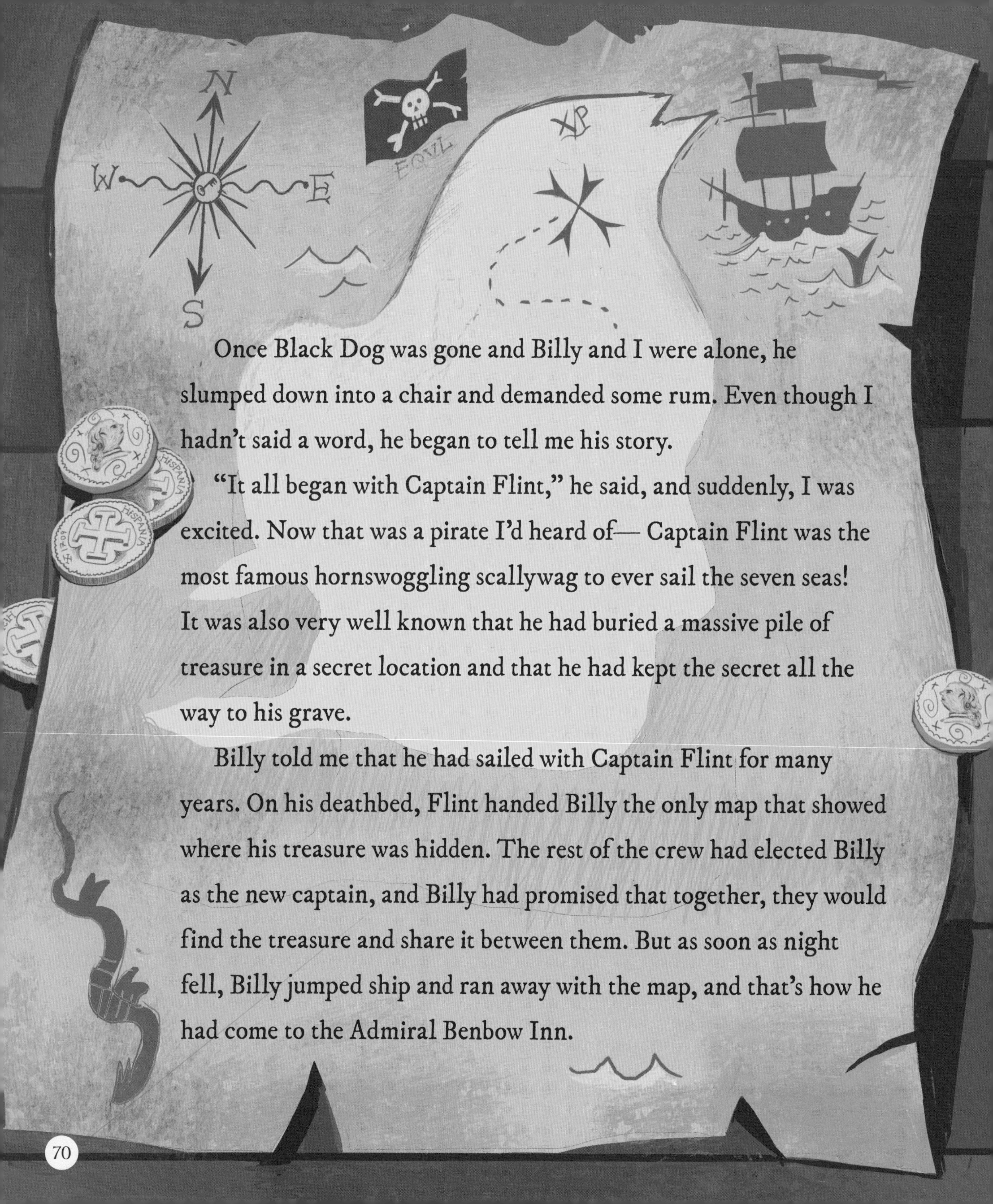

Once Black Dog was gone and Billy and I were alone, he slumped down into a chair and demanded some rum. Even though I hadn't said a word, he began to tell me his story.

"It all began with Captain Flint," he said, and suddenly, I was excited. Now that was a pirate I'd heard of— Captain Flint was the most famous hornswoggling scallywag to ever sail the seven seas! It was also very well known that he had buried a massive pile of treasure in a secret location and that he had kept the secret all the way to his grave.

Billy told me that he had sailed with Captain Flint for many years. On his deathbed, Flint handed Billy the only map that showed where his treasure was hidden. The rest of the crew had elected Billy as the new captain, and Billy had promised that together, they would find the treasure and share it between them. But as soon as night fell, Billy jumped ship and ran away with the map, and that's how he had come to the Admiral Benbow Inn.

“Shiver me timbers, but there’s only one thing for it,” said Billy, wringing his hands together. He was pale with worry. “I’ll have to weigh anchor and clear out of here before ten o’clock.” And with that, he jumped out of his seat and hurried up the stairs.

I must admit, I was glad that Billy was finally leaving, but I was also quite concerned about what would happen to my mother and me when this gang of cut-throat pirates arrived to find Billy gone and the map with him.

But I needn’t have worried about any of that because, as Billy reached the top step, he suddenly turned, clutched at his chest, went as stiff as a statue, then tumbled all the way back down to the bottom of the stairs. He’d been so worried about getting caught that his heart had given out! And so Billy Bones was no more.

My mother, who had been watching and listening from the kitchen, came into the room. "Well, come on, Jim!" she said to me. "We'd better find this map."

The two of us hurried upstairs to Billy's room and pried open the lock on his trunk with a knife. We sifted through everything until we finally found an old piece of parchment at the bottom. My whole body shivered with excitement as I read the heading:

TREASURE ISLAND.

Just then, the clock began to chime ten . . . and between the chimes we heard footsteps outside. We hugged each other in fright.

"We've got to get out of here!" I whispered. I stuffed the map into my shirt, then dragged my mother downstairs, through the kitchen, and out the back door. We went straight into town to the home of our friend, Dr. Livesey.

Dr. Livesey gave us hot tea and listened to our tale with growing excitement. “A real treasure map!” he gasped when we showed him the parchment. “And the famous Captain Flint’s, by Jove! We must show this to Squire Trelawney as soon as possible—he’ll know what to do.”

The following morning we set off to see the squire, who nearly fell off his chair when we showed him the map. And he sure did know what to do—he funded a treasure hunt!

Six weeks later, after much organization and preparation, I was aboard a lovely ship called the *Hispaniola*. Also aboard were Dr. Livesey, Squire Trelawney, and the rest of the crew that the squire had hired. I had been introduced to them all, but I had become closest to the galley cook—a man named Long John Silver.

Silver was rather an odd-looking fellow. He was missing one leg and had a carved wooden stick in its place. He also had a large green parrot that sat on his shoulder and squawked a lot of nonsense, but none of it really made sense to me. Some of its favorite sayings were "Argh, me hearties," "Ahoy, matey," and "Walk the plank!"

Silver told me stories and taught me about life at sea. He always told me I was as "smart as paint." I wasn't sure how smart paint could really be, but we became good friends anyway.

So, one evening I was very surprised to hear Silver and another crew member, Israel Hands, talking quietly.

"When can we finally take over this ship?" asked Israel. "The men are getting restless."

"As soon as we get hold of the map," replied Silver. "Then we'll throw that landlubbing squire and his men overboard and find Flint's treasure!"

I couldn't believe my ears—Silver was a mutinous pirate! Who'd ever heard of a peg-legged pirate with a parrot on his shoulder? As they discussed their plan, I learned that most of the crew on board were Silver's own people.

I waited until Silver and Hands were gone, then I ran straight to the squire's cabin. I told him what I had overheard and he sent me to fetch the other men he knew to be loyal: Dr. Livesey, Captain Smollett, and three others.

Together we discussed the dire situation. The squire spoke: "We can't turn back toward home or the rotten rascals will mutiny. We must make it to the island before they find the map. Luckily, I have it hidden away where they'll never find it." Captain Smollett nodded thoughtfully, and told us he had an idea.

A few days later, we reached the island and dropped anchor. The squire had been right—for all they had tried, the pirates had not been able to find the map. It was time to put the next part of our plan into action.

Silver and his crew were sent ashore to find fresh water and a place to camp, which they were happy to do after a long voyage. They still had no idea that we knew of their treachery, and they expected us to follow a few hours later once we had completed our chores on board.

Instead, as soon as darkness fell, we sailed the ship around to the other side of the island. We knew from the map that there was a small fort there, so we dropped the anchor, loaded as many supplies as we could onto two rowboats, and went ashore.

It wasn't until the next day that Silver realized what we had done and, when he finally found our hideout, he was very angry at having been fooled. We were ready and waiting for the pirates' arrival, knowing that we would have to defend ourselves against a group that was twice our number.

"We have you surrounded!" Silver shouted from the clearing outside the fort. "But I shall leave you all unharmed if you just hand over the map."

The squire shouted back his refusal and the first cracks of gunfire filled the air. Soon everybody was firing wildly, the air was thick with smoke, and splinters of wood were flying everywhere. I did as I was instructed, and ran between each man in the fort, reloading one musket while he fired another.

Eventually the firing outside slowed down, and then stopped all together. I ran to the window and could see nobody outside. "They've gone!" I shouted. "We've won!"

But the captain just shook his head. "They'll be back," he said.

The next day came, but there was no sign of Silver. I was bored of being cooped up in the fort, so I offered to explore the island and spy on the pirate camp.

I headed out of the fort and across the island but, before I could find the pirates, I found something far more extraordinary on the hillside: a strange creature hopping from rock to rock. It moved as nimbly as a mountain goat, but it didn't look like any beast I had seen before. It finally stopped, turned, and stared at me, and then I realized it was a man! He seemed nervous at first, then slowly started to climb closer and closer to where I stood. And then he spoke.

"Got any cheese?" he asked. It wasn't quite what I was expecting him to say, but I did have a piece of cheese wrapped in cloth in my pocket, which I had brought along for my lunch. I pulled it out and offered it to him, and he quickly reached across and snatched it. He took a bite, then he screwed up his face in happiness and leaped from one leg to the other. I waited until he had finished the cheese, then asked him who he was and what he was doing here.

"The name's Ben Gunn," he said, "and I haven't seen another human in three years." Ben explained that he had been marooned on the island. I told him about my friends and the pirates and invited him back to the fort. He refused, but he did ask me to send the doctor out to see him, which I agreed to do.

Back at the fort, the others were very interested in Ben's story. They thought he might even know something helpful about the island or the treasure. Everyone agreed that the doctor should visit him the very next day.

The next morning, all was still quiet, so I decided to go out exploring again. I slipped quietly out of the fort before the others awoke and wandered along the beach, through the forest, and up the hill.

I was having a grand old adventure, until I realized the sun was beginning to set and I was a long way from the fort. I made my way back as quickly as I could, but it was well after dark when I arrived. I was expecting a good telling off from Dr. Livesey, but when I opened the door to the inner hall, all I could hear was snoring.

Relieved, I crept through toward my sleeping mat, but in the dark I managed to trip over a sleeping body. At first I thought it was one of our men, but then out of the darkness I heard a squawk: "Walk the plank!"

Voices yelled in the dark, and someone lit a lantern. I looked around in the dim light and realized that I had tripped over Long John Silver—and the fort was full of his men. There was no escape.

"Well, hello Jim Boy!" said Silver in that fake friendly way of his. "I knew you'd come to your senses and join us. I've always thought you'd make a fine pirate!"

"What have you done with the others?" I demanded.

"Not to worry," said Silver. "We made a little deal earlier today. I got the map, and they got to leave with their lives." He saw that I was puzzled and must have guessed that I was wondering why they had gone without me. Had they forgotten me?

Silver chuckled. "No, my boy, they didn't forget you. When you disappeared, they thought you might have changed sides. I was happy to tell them that was true. Anyway, better get some rest. We're hunting for treasure tomorrow!"

We were up and ready to go early the following morning. Silver read the directions on the map aloud: Start Skeleton Island. Big tree. North-west to Spy Glass Hill. Tall tree. Ten paces south.

From the map, we could see that Skeleton Island was a tiny island that lay alongside the bigger island we were on. We made our way down to the shore and piled into two rowboats. When we reached Skeleton Island, Silver ordered the men to fan out and search for a big tree. He was worried that, given the chance, I would run off, so he brought a rope from the boat, which he tied through my belt to his own to stop me from getting away.

A short while later we heard a shout from within the forest. We rushed toward the sound and were horrified to find Israel Hands standing over a skeleton. It had an eye patch and a tatty blue jacket with a cutlass tucked into the belt. But most strangely of all, while one bony arm was resting by its side, the other was outstretched, as if pointing back to the main island. Silver pulled out his compass and placed it alongside the pointing arm.

"Praise the stars!" said Silver. "This is one of Flint's jokes. He always was a black-hearted joker. If I'm not mistaken, these arm bones are pointing straight to the treasure." Captain Flint had left a skeleton to show us the way.

So, we loaded into the boats and rowed back to Treasure Island. Once we were ashore, we headed toward Spyglass Hill in search of the big tree. I couldn't help but wonder what other surprises Captain Flint might have left for us.

Finally we reached a clump of trees, in the very center of which stood an enormous tree that towered above the rest. Silver rubbed his hands together and did a little jig: well, a sort of jig given he had a peg for a leg. “We’re almost there! It’s so close, I can smell the treasure!”

Flint stood at the base of the tree and held out his compass. “Now for the final clue,” he said. “Ten paces south.” With that, he began counting out the steps. At six he ordered the men to ready their shovels, at eight he was visibly quivering with excitement, but at ten he let out a great cry of anger. We stood at the edge of an enormous pit, and inside the pit was . . . absolutely nothing.

Somebody had already found the treasure!

As we all stood in shocked silence, we heard a voice call out from the tree line. "Stay where you are, you no-good stinking pirates!"

It was Squire Trelawney! He stepped out from the trees, along with Dr. Livesey, Captain Smollett, and Ben Gunn. All the pirates except Silver, who still had me tied to him, bolted for the cover of the trees on the opposite side. The squire let off a musket shot but it went wide and they all got away.

The captain kept his musket aimed at Silver and the doctor rushed over to untie me. He gave me a fond pat on the head. "I'm glad to see you safe and well, Jim!" he said. "We never thought for a moment that you would join the pirates." I couldn't begin to describe my relief!

The doctor told us what had happened while I was out exploring: "I went to see Ben Gunn, and learned that he had dug up the treasure and hidden it somewhere else. That made the map useless, so I gave it to you, Silver. After all, you did say you wanted it. Then we set up this ambush and waited for you to come to us."

Silver scowled, and the doctor seemed quite pleased with himself.

The next morning, Ben took us to the treasure, which he had hidden in a cave down by the beach. I don't think any of us were truly prepared for the huge fortune Captain Flint had collected: there were rows upon rows of gold bars, chests full of gold coins, and others overflowing with jewels! While the rest of us were awed, Silver seemed distraught by the amount of treasure that could have been his. I could swear I even saw a tear slide from the corner of his eye and down his cheek.

We spent all that day loading the treasure onto rowboats and out to the *Hispaniola.* We had the treasure and we were going home!

Silver was to come with us. He would be taken back home and charged with piracy. We would leave the other pirates marooned on the island. Ben Gunn assured us that would be as harsh a punishment as any. We left them some food and supplies on the beach before we made our final trip out to board the ship and set sail. They would never cause trouble on the high seas again.

After a few weeks at sea, we pulled into a busy port for fresh water. We left Ben Gunn onboard to watch over Long John Silver and went ashore. When we climbed back aboard at the end of the day, I noticed that Silver was not in his usual spot on the deck. I asked Ben where he was and Ben, rather sheepishly, admitted he had let Silver escape. We were all outraged at first, but then Ben explained: "I could see him sitting there plotting, day after day. He would not have rested until he found a way to take the ship and steal the treasure. I gave him a bag of gold and sent him on his way before anyone was hurt."

After everything Silver had done, we all supposed Ben was probably right, so we set off on the last leg of our extraordinary journey.

When we finally docked at our home port, all I could think about was seeing my mother! I picked up the heavy sack that contained my cut of the treasure and raced down the gangplank and up the street on wobbly legs that weren't used to being back on land.

I hired the first carriage I saw to take me to the Admiral Benbow Inn as fast as the horses could take us. When we finally reached the inn, I saw my mother sweeping the front doorstep. She stopped when she saw me and a smile lit up her face.

I ran to the front door and swept my mother into a hug, twirling her around and planting a giant kiss on her forehead. "Did you miss me, Ma?" I asked, and she simply cried. But when I showed her what was in my sack, she began to laugh and I hugged her again. I was so very glad to be home, and decided I was more than happy to be a regular landlubber for the rest of my days.

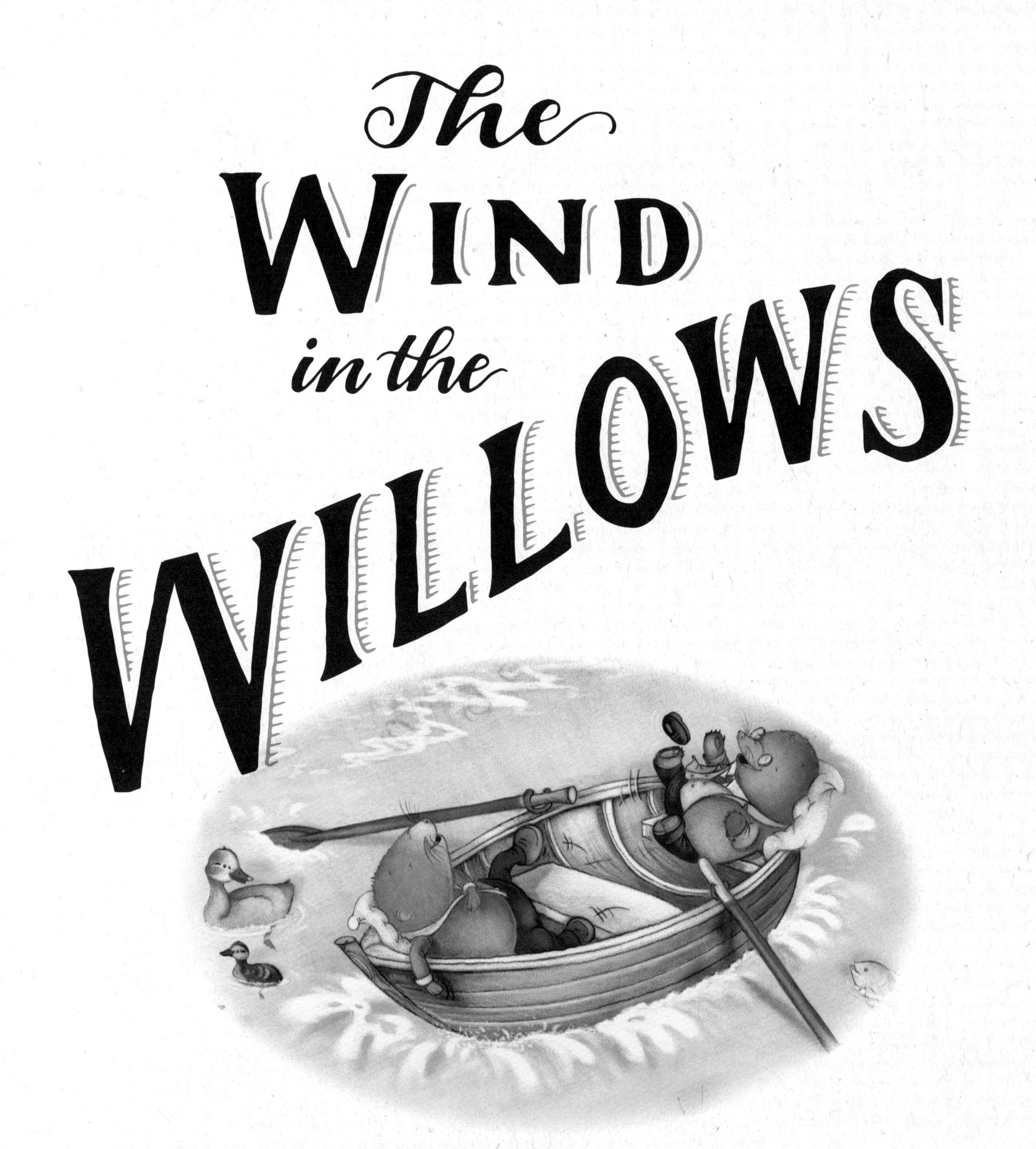

Based on the original story by

KENNETH GRAHAME

Mole had spent all morning spring-cleaning his little home. He had dust in his throat and eyes, splashes of paint over his black fur, an aching back, and tired arms. Mole flung his brush on the floor. "Hang spring-cleaning!" he said, and he marched out the front door, up the tunnel, and into the sunshine.

Mole ran and tumbled through the warm grass. He ran and ran, through meadows and small woods, until he came to a wide river that was all a-shake and a-shiver, glinting in the sun. He sat down by the bank, fascinated. Mole had never traveled this far from home, and he'd never seen a river. He didn't feel at all guilty about leaving his spring-cleaning behind.

Just then, Mole saw a dark hole in the opposite bank. In that hole, looking back at him, were two bright eyes! Mole waved and soon a little brown creature with a friendly face and long whiskers emerged. It was a water rat!

"Hello, Mole," said the water rat.

"Hello, Rat," replied Mole.

"Would you like to come over?" asked Rat.

"I sure would!" said Mole.

Rat got into a little green boat and rowed across the river. Mole climbed in— a rather tricky business as Mole's short arms and legs made this quite difficult. Rat pulled and heaved until eventually Mole tumbled over the side and they both fell in a heap at the bottom of the boat, giggling.

Rat began to row and Mole felt he'd never been so happy in his life. "What a wonderful day this is!" he said.

Rat agreed. "Believe me," he said, "there is nothing better than simply messing about in boats. Shall we make a day of it?"

"Oh, yes please!" replied Mole.

Before they set off, Rat stopped at his house and climbed back on board with a large basket. "What's inside?" asked Mole.

"Oh, just cold chicken," replied Rat, rowing away from the bank, "and a leg of ham, cold beef, fruit salad, bread rolls, sandwiches, ginger beer, lemonade, chocolate cake . . . "

Mole couldn't believe his ears. What a feast! He trailed a paw in the water and daydreamed until they bumped gently against the riverbank.

They had a delightful lunch, watching the activity on the busy river. At one point, Rat waved as his good friend Toad passed by in a brand-new rowboat.

Mole thought it was a wonderful boat. "Oh, it won't last long," replied Rat. "Toad will crash it or break it, and by this time next week he'll have a new toy or hobby. Toad is a very fine fellow but he's quite irresponsible, and a terrible braggart."

Rat regaled Mole with Toad's adventures for the rest of the afternoon. When it was time to leave, Rat invited Mole to stay at his house for a while. Mole was delighted—Rat had even promised to teach him to row and to swim. What grand adventures the fast friends would have!

One bright summer morning, Mole said, "Ratty, can I ask you a favor?"

"Of course my dear fellow," replied Rat, who was splashing in the river.

"Would you take me to see Toad? I would so like to meet him."

"Certainly!" said Rat. "Let's get the boat and set out at once. Toad's always happy to have visitors."

And indeed, Toad was. He rushed out to meet them on the rolling green lawn. "Welcome to Toad Hall!" he called, waving his arm toward the sprawling brick mansion.

Mole told Toad how much he admired Toad Hall. "It's the finest house on the river, isn't it?" boasted Toad. "In fact, it's the finest house anywhere!"

Mole asked Toad how he was enjoying his new boat. "Oh, boats-shmoats!" replied Toad. "I'm over boats. I have a new passion—caravanning!"

Toad excitedly dragged them to show off his very fancy new caravan. "Tomorrow I am taking off on a long journey. I might be gone weeks, or even years! You should join me," he suggested.

Rat quickly thanked Toad but declined his invitation. He had been on adventures with Toad before, and they never turned out well.

After a lovely day, Mole and Rat headed home, wishing Toad happy travels.

One day, Rat was teaching Mole to swim when there was a rustle in the bushes and a striped head appeared.

"Oh, hello Badger!" called Rat. "Won't you come and join us?" But the creature quickly disappeared without saying a word.

Mole was puzzled until Rat explained that Badger was very shy. This made Mole very curious to meet Badger, so he asked Rat if they could visit him. "We simply can't. Badger lives in the Wild Wood, which is a dark and unfriendly place," warned Rat.

At first Mole accepted this but, as the days wore on and winter arrived, he felt he absolutely had to meet Badger. One afternoon while Rat was resting, Mole slipped out and headed for the Wild Wood. The wind was blowing, and the Wood was very dark and gloomy, especially as night began to set in.

Mole began to feel quite scared. There were glowing eyes staring at him from trees and bushes, and suddenly a rabbit rushed past him. "Get out of here!" the rabbit cried. "The Wild Wood is full of dangerous stoats and weasels!"

Mole began to panic. He ran about blindly, tripping over tree roots and crashing into other creatures until he found a hollow in an old tree. He crept inside, shivering and shaking and wishing he'd listened to Rat.

Back home, Rat had awoken from his nap to find Mole missing. He looked outside and saw footprints in the snow leading to the Wild Wood. Rat knew exactly where Mole had gone. He pulled on a warm coat, lit a lantern, and headed out to find his friend.

Rat followed the footprints all through the Wood until he reached the tree hollow. He held the lantern up and found Mole inside, terrified but safe.

"Oh, Moly!" said Rat. "I was terribly worried. Let's get you home." But it had started snowing, so when they tried to retrace their footsteps, they found the snow had covered them over. Mole and Rat were helplessly lost.

They blundered through the cold, wet snow for hours. "Oh, we're going to freeze out here if starvation doesn't get us first!" cried Mole. "And only if we don't get carried off by wild creatures!"

Mole grew so tired that his little legs could scarcely carry him and he tripped over a stone. As he sat in the cold snow rubbing his shin, Rat suddenly let out a whoop of delight.

"Well done Moly!" Rat cried. "You've stumbled onto Badger's doorstep!" They cleared the snow from around the doorstep and soon came to a small green door and a bell, which Rat happily rang. They heard slow footsteps approaching the door and it eventually opened just wide enough to a reveal a long snout and a pair of sleepy eyes.

"Badger! Please let us in! It's me, Water Rat, and my new friend Mole. We're lost in the snow."

"Ratty, my dear little man!" exclaimed Badger. "Come in at once. You must be freezing."

Inside, Badger sat Rat and Mole in front of the fire and gave them warm dressing gowns, slippers, and cups of hot chocolate. As they warmed through, Badger asked them what was new on the riverbank.

"Oh, it's much the same," replied Rat. "Toad has given up caravanning and taken up driving motor cars. He really is the worst driver—he's crashed seven cars already! It won't be long before someone gets hurt."

"Well, we can't be expected to do anything strenuous, or heroic, or even moderately active during winter," said Badger, yawning. "But I tell you what, Ratty. When the weather is warmer, we'll go to Toad and make him see sense. But now it's bedtime."

Soon the snow cleared and the sun peeked out from behind the clouds. It was spring once more.

One morning, Badger arrived at Rat's house. "It's time to pay Toad a visit," he announced. "He has just bought himself a new, very powerful motor car. We must convince him to give up his dangerous ways."

The three friends set off to Toad Hall and spotted the shiny new car parked outside. Toad flung open the front door cheerfully.

"Hello, hello!" he shouted. "Have you come to see my new motor car? I do believe it is the most splendid car in the whole world. You're just in time for a drive!"

"It seems we are just in time, but not for a drive," said Badger. He dragged Toad inside to the study. After a while, they came back out and Badger announced that Toad had agreed to change his irresponsible ways and give up motor cars forever.

Toad wriggled and writhed for a moment, then cried, "I won't! I love driving! It's so much fun and I'll drive as fast as I like!"

Badger angrily told Toad he would have to stay in his room until he saw reason, and confiscated Toad's car keys.

Later that day, when the house had gone quiet, Toad climbed out the window and down the drainpipe. He ran until he came to a small town where he saw a shiny motor car parked by the road. The keys were inside! Toad couldn't help himself—he climbed in, started the engine, and took off with a screech. He was soon out in the countryside with the engine roaring and the wind whipping past. He was so happy! At least, that is, until disaster struck.

A few days later, Toad found himself in court in handcuffs, charged with stealing a motor car, driving dangerously, and crashing into a ditch. Toad was convinced he would simply be given a fine, but the stern judge had something else in mind.

"I sentence you to twenty years in jail!" he boomed.

Toad was shocked and, all of a sudden, very sorry for his bad behavior.

"I'm sorry!" he wailed. "Take pity on a poor Toad who didn't know any better!" But it was too late. The guards dragged him away and locked him in a cold, gray cell.

Days passed and Toad felt very sorry for himself indeed. How he wished he had listened to his friends! "Wise Badger, clever Rat, sensible Mole," he said to himself. "You tried to save me from myself but I wouldn't listen. I swear, if I ever get out of here, I will be a much better Toad!"

Toad sounded so sad and sorry that the jailor's daughter, who often brought food to the prisoners, felt terribly bad for him and offered to help him escape. Toad was overjoyed, and ever so thankful.

The girl brought Toad some clothes to disguise himself so that he could sneak out. Toad thought he might dress as a great lord, but was very disappointed when he found he was to dress as a washerwoman. The girl helped him pull on a long dress, an apron, and a bonnet that covered most of his face, and when all was in place, Toad slipped out to make his escape.

The runaway washerwoman headed for the station and boarded the next train. Toad sat down and chuckled to himself. "What an extraordinary Toad I am!" he thought to himself. "Who else but me could escape from such a place!"

But soon enough, Toad was in hot water again: he could hear sirens following the train and he knew that the police would catch up to him. "What a silly Toad I am," he wailed, panicking. "Of course the police would find me here! What am I to do?"

Toad needed to get off without being seen, so he waited until the train went through a tunnel, and jumped out on the other side. He landed with a crash and tumbled down the hill into a bush. The sirens passed without slowing, and Toad realized he wasn't going to get caught. He brushed himself off, then skipped along, singing a song he'd just made up called "What a Clever Toad Am I."

After a while, Toad came to a river. He followed it, still dressed as a washerwoman and singing away. Soon he heard the clip-clopping of a horse walking along the riverbank behind him. It was pulling a barge along the river. Toad felt quite tired, and fancied a comfortable ride on the barge. He asked the woman steering it if he could come aboard.

"Do you have money to pay for your passage?" she asked.

"Alas, I do not!" he cried in a high-pitched voice. "I am just a poor washerwoman. Do take pity on me!"

The woman guided the barge to the bank and Toad hopped on.

Toad was quite pleased with himself until he realized that the woman had absolutely no intention of giving him a free ride.

"Lucky for you," the woman said to Toad, "I have a gigantic, enormous, stupendous pile of laundry below deck that needs washing. Hop to it!" And she gave him a little shove down a short staircase.

Toad would never dream of doing such hard work, so he decided to take a nap on the washing pile. Soon enough, the woman found him fast asleep.

She flew into a rage. "Lazy cheat!" the woman cried. She pushed Toad up the stairs, picked him up, and threw him straight over the side! He landed in the river with a huge splash.

Toad coughed and spluttered and kicked and paddled until he reached the bank. He was a soggy mess, and now he was really quite furious. He hopped up and down and shook his fist in the air. "I'll teach you to mess with the famous Mr. Toad!" he shouted.

He ran along the riverbank until he caught up with the barge horse. Ignoring the woman's angry cries, he untied the horse, mounted it, and galloped away, laughing like a madman as he sang his latest ditty, "Ain't No Better Toad than Toad."

But Toad soon found that a horse without a saddle makes for quite a tender backside, so he decided to set the horse free. He climbed down, rubbing his sore bottom, and continued along the river on foot.

By now, the light was beginning to fade and Toad was tired and hungry. He didn't want to spend the night out in the open and began to worry. "Why, oh why do dreadful things always happen to poor Toad?" he asked himself, plopping down on a rock beside the river.

Just then a motor car came along the road beside the river. Two men in the car saw someone who they took to be a poor washerwoman beside the road and pulled over to see if they could help.

"Oh, thank you, kind gentlemen," said Toad in his high-pitched washerwoman's voice, and they were soon traveling down the road. But the driver wasn't going fast enough for Toad's liking, so he asked, "Would you be so kind as to allow me to drive? I have always dreamed of driving a motor car." The men thought this an odd request, but they were polite fellows, so they agreed.

But once Toad was behind the wheel, he was a menace! He took off, speeding around corners so fast that two wheels lifted off the ground. The men were terrified, holding on for dear life and yelling for Toad to slow down. Eventually, Toad's bonnet blew off his head.

"You!" cried one of the shocked men. "You're that escaped prisoner!"

"Yes, it is I, Toad!" said Toad, "The motor-car snatcher, the prison breaker, the Toad who always escapes!" The men tried to grab Toad, but he suddenly pulled hard on the steering wheel, sending the car right over the edge of the riverbank. Toad was flung high and far, landing on the other side of the river.

He stood on the far bank watching the men struggling out of the river and began to giggle—as much as they might try, no one got the better of Toad! Toad realized he had almost made it to Ratty's house, so he tramped along merrily, composing a new song called "Ode to Toad."

Toad was overjoyed when he found his good friends Mole and Ratty at home, and they were most relieved to see their friend safe and well. Toad told them how he'd outsmarted everyone who was after him and he'd even begun to sing one of his new songs when Ratty cut him short.

"Enough!" said Rat. "Stop bragging, go upstairs, and change out of those ridiculous clothes. Come back down looking like a gentleman, if you can. Then we should talk."

Toad was very surprised at Ratty's tone, but he did what he was told, mumbling under his breath about someone being a bossy-boots.

When Toad came back downstairs, Mole gave him a plate of supper. Rat looked very serious. "From what you've told me, you've been handcuffed, imprisoned, terrified out of your mind, starved, chased, and flung into a river," he said. "And all because you just had to steal a motor car. What is there to be proud of?"

Toad could see Rat's point when he put it like that. He felt quite foolish and promised Rat and Mole he would not mess about with motor cars again. He felt very tired and told them he was going home to sleep in his own bed.

Mole sighed sadly, and Rat said, "Oh dear, Toady, haven't you heard? The weasels and ferrets have taken over Toad Hall, and they refuse to leave."

It made Toad angry to think of his beautiful house overrun by wild creatures, eating his food, touching his things, and sleeping in his bed. "I must take it back!" he said.

Just then there was a knock on the door, and Mole opened it to find Badger outside. He came in and shook Toad's hand firmly. "My dear Toady," he said, "I'm so glad to see you safe and well! But what are we going to do about this Toad Hall business?" Toad was very relieved that his friends were willing to help, and the four creatures spent the evening hatching a plan.

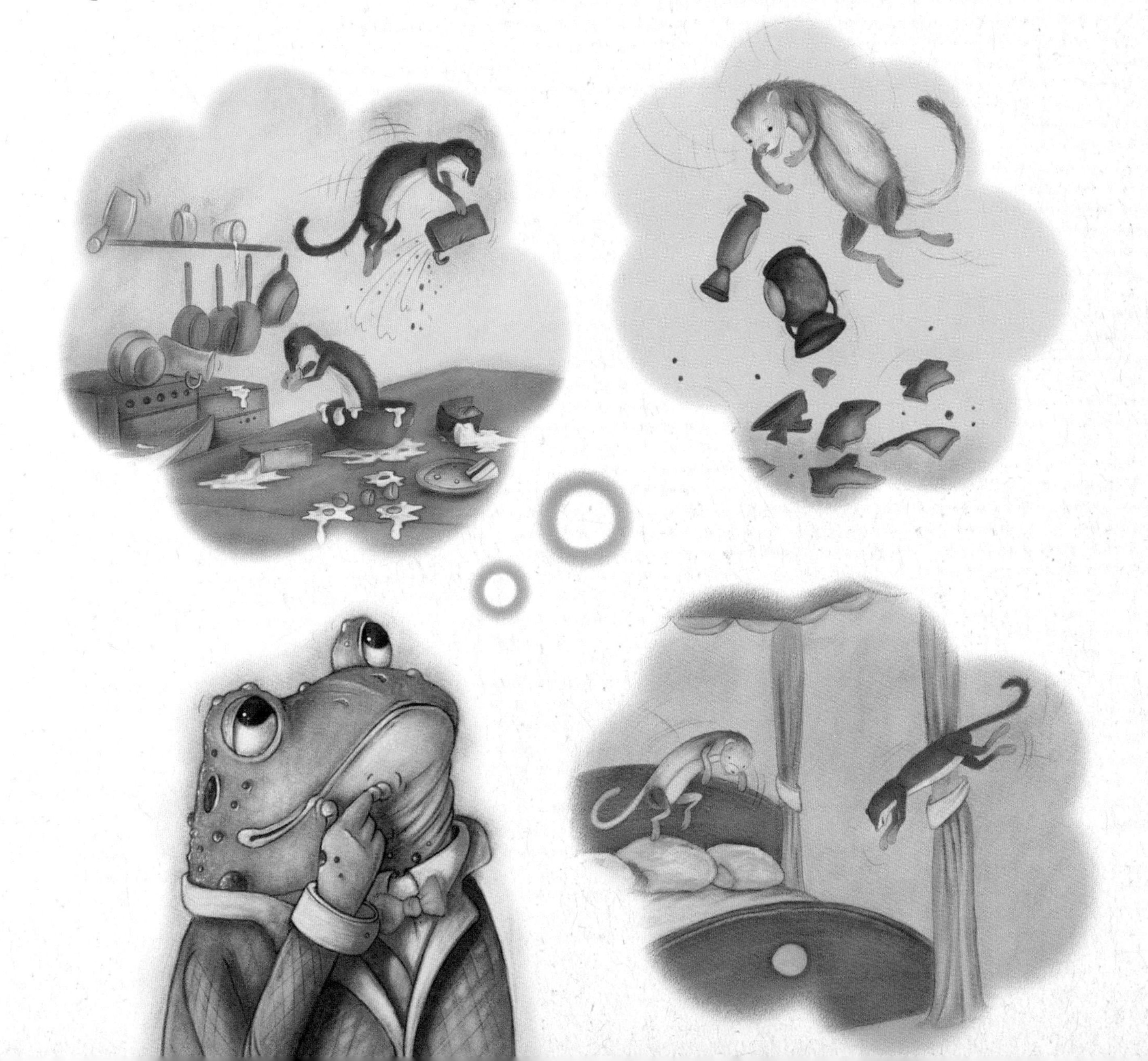

The following evening, the Chief Weasel was throwing a birthday party at Toad Hall. Badger thought this would be the perfect opportunity to sneak into Toad's house. They crept to the edge of the property and Toad guided them through a secret underground passage into the cellar, directly below the banquet hall. Each of them carried a long stick to fight off the wild creatures once they were inside.

"Right," said Badger when they reached the cellar. "Once we're up the stairs, we'll burst into the hall and take them by surprise."

“Then we’ll whack ’em and whack ’em and whack ’em!” cried Toad, hopping up and down. “Let’s go!”

The four friends rushed into the banquet hall, screaming and squawking and waving their sticks around. The weasels, stoats, and ferrets were so surprised at the raucous display that they thought a whole army had invaded the hall. They dropped their food and dashed out of Toad Hall as fast as their legs could carry them!

Ratty, Badger, Mole, and Toad all cheered, then rewarded themselves by finishing the banquet.

From that day forward, Toad was a changed creature. He sent money and letters of thanks for their help and apologies for his poor behavior to the jailor's daughter, the lady from the barge, and the two gentlemen whose car he crashed. He even kept his promise and never drove a motor car again.

Toad always had to try very hard not to brag, but at least he did try. And he only ever sang his newest song, "Toad the Wise and Wonderful," when he thought nobody could hear. Badger, Rat, and Mole who, in fact, heard him quite often, smiled to themselves as they went about their happy, peaceful lives.

Based on the original story by

ANNA SEWELL

The first home I can ever remember was a lovely lush green meadow owned by Farmer Gray. I lived there with my mother, Duchess, who was the master's favorite. I spent my younger days frolicking in the fields, splashing in the pond, and playing with the other colts. It was a wonderful life.

One day, as we were playing a rough game that involved a lot of kicking and biting, my mother called me to her. She told me: "The other colts that live here are not bad creatures, but they have never learned manners. To grow into a proud and respectable stallion, you must do your work without complaining, lift your feet high when you trot, and never ever kick or bite."

My mother was wise, so I took her advice to heart.

Soon after, Farmer Gray decided that I was old enough to learn to be a working horse. I needed to learn how to pull a cart or a carriage and to have people ride on my back. This training was called my "breaking in"—and it wasn't fun at all!

I had to wear a bridle, which was made of straps that went around my head and under my nose and chin. I didn't like that very much. And I had to wear a bit, which was a metal rod that was placed in my mouth and attached to the bridle and reins. That was the worst! If I didn't turn my head the right way when my master pulled on the reins, the bit would hurt my mouth.

But my master was kind and gentle, and soon I learned what he needed me to do. I actually felt quite proud carrying him around on my back—what a grown-up horse I had become!

When I was four years old (which meant I was fully grown), it was time for Farmer Gray to sell me. One day, a man named Squire Gordon came to the farm. He picked up my feet and checked my hoofs and he opened my mouth and looked at my teeth. It was very tempting to give the cheeky chap a quick nip, but I remembered what my mother had taught me, and he decided he liked what he saw.

I was excited to see what my new life would bring, but I was very sad to say goodbye to my mother and Farmer Gray. I nuzzled them both and whinnied a soft farewell as I was led away.

Squire Gordon lived on a big fancy farm with a pretty white house and wonderfully spacious, bright, tidy stables. That was where I met John, the groom, and Joe, the stable boy. They both looked me over and agreed I was as fine a horse as ever they saw. I liked them both immediately, though I could

tell Joe was young and didn't know a lot about horses. They brushed me and fed me a bucket of oats and led me into a comfortable stall spread with fresh straw.

"The Squire says you're to be called Black Beauty," Joe said as he patted me gently on the nose. I felt very proud to have such a grand name!

Once they left, I looked around and realized I was not alone. In the stall beside me was a stout little gray pony, who introduced himself as Merrylegs. "I'm very important around here," he told me proudly. "I am responsible for teaching the Squire's two little daughters."

"Teaching them what?" I asked, puzzled.

"To ride horses, of course!" he answered. Well, I had heard of people training horses but never of horses training people! What a funny place this was.

"I let them ride on my back, but if they are silly or misbehave, then I give a little buck and they fall right off into the mud—and that teaches them!" he explained.

That was when I heard a snort from another stall at the back of the stable and I looked around to see a chestnut mare in the far corner. She was eyeing me angrily.

"Oh, don't worry about Ginger," Merrylegs told me. "She likes to tease me because she secretly fancies me. I am quite irresistible, you see." I wasn't sure I believed him, but I liked Merrylegs immediately.

Ginger rolled her large eyes at us and turned away. I found out later that Ginger was very grumpy because I had been given her stall. She had bitten one of the master's children and they had become frightened of her.

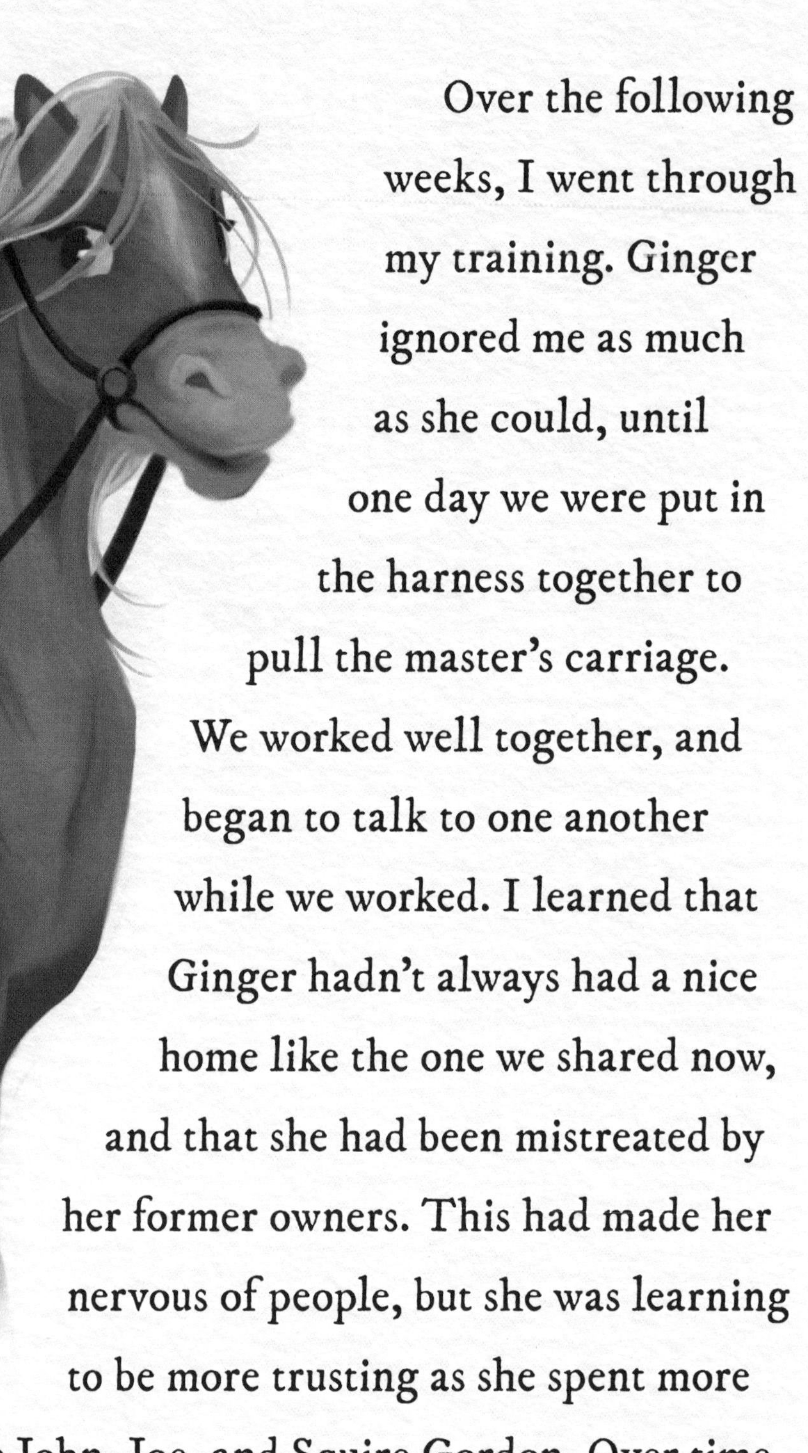

Over the following weeks, I went through my training. Ginger ignored me as much as she could, until one day we were put in the harness together to pull the master's carriage. We worked well together, and began to talk to one another while we worked. I learned that Ginger hadn't always had a nice home like the one we shared now, and that she had been mistreated by her former owners. This had made her nervous of people, but she was learning to be more trusting as she spent more time with kind and gentle folk like John, Joe, and Squire Gordon. Over time we became good friends.

One day, as Ginger and I were bringing John home from town, I saw my first example of a horse being treated badly. Bill Bushby, a man who worked for the neighbor, was trying to force his pony to jump a gate that was clearly too high for him. The pony refused to jump, so Bill climbed from the saddle and began to whip him, and when the pony still refused to jump, Bill began to kick him.

This made John furious! He leaped out of the carriage to put a stop to Bill's terrible treatment of the pony when, all of a sudden, the pony put his head down and threw up his heels, kicking bratty Bill up into the air. He went up and up, then seemed to freeze in mid-air before he came tumbling back down like a sack of potatoes, landing right in a thorny blackberry bush.

Bill scrambled around untangling himself from the bush as the pony took off toward home at a gallop. Billy followed behind, yelling, "Ouch, ouch, ouch!" and pulling thorns out of his backside as he ran.

"Well, that fixes that!" chuckled John and climbed back into the carriage. He even made sure to tell the neighbor what had happened so the poor pony wouldn't be in trouble, and I liked John even more after that.

One day during winter, John harnessed me to a small cart. I was to take him and Squire Gordon into town on some urgent business. It had been raining for many days and when we reached the wooden bridge that crossed the river, the water was rising fast.

"We'll have to return as quickly as we can before this bridge is flooded," warned John, and Squire Gordon nodded his agreement. But because the country roads were slick with mud, the wind was howling, and the rain was pouring, it took a long time to reach the town. By the time Squire Gordon had completed his business and we had made it back to the bridge, the water was even higher, with a few inches of water covering the center of the bridge.

"Drive on," said Squire Gordon. "We'll make it across if we hurry."

John gave me a light touch with his whip and urged me on, but the moment I took my first step onto the bridge, I came to a dead stop. I knew something was wrong.

"Crack the whip, John," said Squire Gordon. "We need to get across fast." John urged me on again, but still I wouldn't budge. I could tell the Squire was becoming cross with me.

"There's something wrong, sir," John said. Of course, I couldn't tell him, but I knew the bridge wasn't safe. At that very moment, there came a terrible crack like the sound of thunder and the whole center section of the bridge tore away and was washed downstream.

John and the Squire were shocked. "You clever horse, Beauty," said Squire Gordon. "If you had taken us over that bridge, we all would have been washed into the river and drowned."

Both John and the Squire were very pleased with me, and when we finally reached home I was given a huge supper of bran, crushed beans, and oats. John even had Joe make an extra-thick bed of straw for me, for which I was very grateful, as I'd never been so tired in my life.

Those days at Squire Gordon's farm were very happy ones. Ginger, Merrylegs, and I worked hard, but we were treated well and often had time to play in the meadow. We would chase each other across the field, roll around in the long grass, and even wade into the pond on hot days.

Merrylegs would even have Ginger in stitches as he pranced around the field showing us how fine a stallion he would make for a lord or lady. Merrylegs was only half our size, and so would never be able to carry anyone larger than a small child. He would trot around on his short stumpy legs, then stop to pose with one hoof in the air.

Late one afternoon, while we were frolicking in the field, John came running to the fence and called to me urgently. I galloped to the gate and he led me to the stable.

"It's the mistress," he said as he placed the saddle on my back, and I wondered why he always spoke to me even though he didn't know that I could understand him. "She's very ill and we must fetch the doctor. We must ride faster than we've ever ridden before!"

Once I was ready to go, he leaped up onto my back and I galloped out of the stable and towards the doctor's house. That day I ran like the wind. John didn't need to use the whip because he knew I was running as fast as my legs could carry me. We traveled for miles, passed over a hill, went through a village, clattered over a rickety bridge, and passed another village before we finally reached the doctor's house. It was late and the air was cool when we arrived.

John banged on the door and the doctor answered. When John told him of the emergency, the doctor was quite troubled. "My horse is lame and I can't take him out," he explained. "I have no way of getting to Mrs. Gordon."

"Take Black Beauty!" said John. "He's tired, but I'm sure he's got the heart to get you there in quick time." The doctor quickly fetched his bag, and John handed over the reins.

I raced back home as fast as I could. My heart was pounding, my breathing was short, and my legs were tired, but I wouldn't let my master down. When we finally reached home, the doctor raced inside and Joe, who had been pulled from his bed, led me back to the stables and into my stall.

I was shaking and panting and had sweat running down my sides. Joe, who was still learning how to care for horses, didn't know what to do. I needed a blanket to keep me warm so that I could cool down slowly, but Joe gave me a bucket of icy water and some hay, then went back to bed.

The next morning, when John arrived home and came to check on me, I was very ill. My shaking had grown worse and I was icy cold. I had developed a fever. John was very angry with Joe. He told Joe that I might die, and Joe began to sob. Joe was very sorry and promised he would do everything he could to nurse me back to health.

Joe lived up to his promise. He fed me and brushed me and talked to me every day and we became the best of friends. Soon I was well enough to go back into the meadow, but it was many months before I was well enough to work again. Mrs. Gordon had shaken off her illness but she was very frail, and the doctor advised that the family move to a warmer climate so her health could improve.

So, the family packed up the house and got ready to leave. Sadly, we horses were not to go with them. John organized a new home for Ginger and me with a grand lord and lady who lived in a big manor house close by. Merrylegs was sold to the local minister, who had two young boys. He said he was very jealous of Ginger and I, and could not understand why he wasn't chosen to pull a fancy lord's carriage.

We all said a very sad goodbye to the Squire and his family, and especially to John and Joe, and Ginger and I left to begin a new life.

Unfortunately for us, it wasn't the kind of life we had been hoping for.

Soon after arriving at our new home, a grand estate owned by Lord and Lady White, I was introduced to a cruel contraption called a bearing rein. The bearing rein was attached to the top of my bridle, and then pulled tight so that my head was yanked up and back into quite an uncomfortable position. Ginger was very upset when our new groom, York, tried to place it on her, as she had endured the bearing rein before. York, who was a kind man, calmed Ginger and told her that he would not pull the rein too tight.

Once we were harnessed, York pulled the carriage around to the front of the house, where the sour-faced Lady White waited to climb aboard. She was angry when she saw us. "Pull those reins tighter!" she snapped at York. "You can't expect me to be seen in town with my horses' heads practically scraping the ground – how vulgar! What would people think?"

York gently tightened the bearing rein, pulling our heads up even higher. It was becoming quite painful!

"Tighter, tighter, tighter!" shrilled Lady White. York tried to argue, but the Lady wouldn't hear of it, so he tightened the rein until my neck hurt terribly and I found it very difficult to breathe.

"Much better," said Lady White and climbed into the carriage. That trip into town was awful. Ginger and I were in pain: we couldn't breathe properly and our legs felt weak. But still Lady White instructed York to whip us to make us go faster.

When we arrived home and finally had our harnesses removed, York brushed us down, gave us food and water, and patted our noses. We knew he felt terrible about the way he'd had to treat us. "I'd like to put a brace around her neck and give her a sound whipping!" he said as he worked. "I can't believe someone would so mistreat a horse for the sake of fashion." I couldn't believe it either.

We worked wearing the bearing rein for a long time and when we weren't working, we were stuck in our stalls. There was no frolicking in the field any more.

Finally, Ginger couldn't take it anymore. One day when a stable boy tried to put the bearing rein on her, she reared, kicked, and lunged at him. She was no longer allowed to pull a carriage afterwards, and instead she was given to Lord White's son to ride.

One day, a groom and I went into the village on an errand and we didn't leave again until well after dark. The groom didn't notice my shoe was loose and, as we rode, it came off. He whipped me to go faster and I tried, but my foot was very sore. At last I stumbled and fell, hurting my knees terribly.

York did his best to help me recover, but I was no longer fit to pull a fancy carriage, so I was sent to the horse market. I was only able to whinny a quick farewell to Ginger, who was very poorly: she had been ridden too hard, which had damaged her lungs and back.

At the horse market, I was placed in a pen with many other horses and buyers came to inspect us. They checked our eyes and teeth and legs, and soon the auction started and we were sold one by one. When it was my turn, several people bid, and I was glad that it was a friendly-looking fellow who finally bought me.

I soon found out that my new job was to pull a cab in London. I had lived my whole life in the countryside with sweet grass in the meadows and the smell of jasmine in the air. When I reached London, I couldn't believe my nostrils! It was like rotten eggs, dead fish, and stinky socks all rolled into one putrid smell! It made my eyes water but my new master, Jerry, didn't even seem to notice the stink.

Jerry lived on a quiet lane with a small but cozy stable at the back of his cottage. Jerry was a kind master who looked after me very well, and his wife Polly and their children would often bring me little treats. I felt like part of their family.

Pulling a cab was hard work but I always did my best for Jerry, just like my mother taught me. We came to know each other very well and with a few words or a gentle pull on the rein, I could tell what he wanted me to do, so he never, ever had to use his whip.

Not all cab horses were as lucky as I was, and I found this out one wintry day when we pulled up beside another cab. The first thing I noticed was that the cab was driven by a squinty-eyed cabby who looked decidedly cruel. I looked to the front of the cab and saw an old, scrawny, exhausted chestnut mare who looked like she was about to collapse. I felt very sorry for the poor creature and I neighed hello. She turned her head, looked at me with sad eyes, and said, "Hello, Beauty."

At first, I was puzzled that she knew my name and then, with a shock, I realized it was Ginger. Poor Ginger! I put my head against hers and we stayed like that until Jerry called out for me to start moving. I didn't want to leave Ginger, but I had to obey my master, so we pulled away.

After that, I often thought sadly of Ginger and hoped that she had moved on to better pastures. I also thought about happy little Merrylegs, who had always made me laugh, and wondered what had become of him.

I stayed with Jerry for many years and lived a happy life, but Jerry was getting old and finally it was time for him to retire. The family was very sad to say goodbye, but they couldn't afford to keep me, so back to the horse market I went.

I was no longer as young and strong and fit as I used to be, so when I arrived at the market, I was placed in a pen at the back with other horses who were old or sick or frail. I worried about what kind of owner would buy me next.

When the auction started and it was my turn to be sold, I was horrified to see Ginger's owner, the squinty-eyed cabby, place a bid on me. Nobody else seemed interested in buying me and I was sure I was facing a life as dreadful as Ginger's. The man climbed onto the fence and grinned at me and, for the first time in my life, I was tempted to bite and kick and run away.

But then someone called through the crowd, and it was the greatest sound I had ever heard in my life—I recognized that voice!

"I'll pay double!" it said, and I looked around to see my old friend Joe at the fence. He was a grown man now, but I would have known him anywhere. I ran to the fence and nuzzled his face while he patted my head and told me how much he'd missed me.

The cruel cabby threw his hat on the ground and stomped up and down, then picked it up and stormed off, muttering under his breath, which made Joe laugh.

A few hours later, we were trotting down the road and I began to recognize the countryside; we were heading back towards Squire Gordon's old farm, and I was overjoyed. Joe could sense my excitement as we entered through the gate and he leaned over and whispered in my ear, "Welcome home, Beauty."

I love my life on the farm with Joe. I work when he needs me to, but otherwise I spend my days grazing in the meadow—I'm too old for frolicking now—and wading in the pond. And best of all, Joe has promised I will have a home here, with him, forever.

Based on the original story by

L. FRANK BAUM

Dorothy was worried. She stood at the front door and looked out across the dusty gray Kansas prairie. A great wind howled, coming ever closer. The shutters rattled and the little wooden house groaned around her.

Dorothy lived with Uncle Henry and Aunt Em, who were both out working in the fields, nowhere to be seen. Dorothy's little gray dog Toto began to whine, so she picked him up and held him in her arms.

As the great wind raced toward her, it whipped up a dust storm. The house shook and shuddered. Within seconds, the house had filled with wind and then Dorothy felt it lift off the ground and whirl up into the sky!

The little house spun through the air for what seemed like hours, until eventually Dorothy felt it falling. It hit the ground with a great thud. Holding Toto in her arms, Dorothy slowly walked outside. She was shocked at what she saw!

The house had landed in a strange and beautiful land, unlike anywhere Dorothy had ever seen. It was so very bright and beautiful! Tall trees groaned under the weight of ripe fruit and nearby a babbling brook ran past, its banks covered with colorful flowers.

Coming toward her was a group of small, odd-looking people. A much older lady in a stunning sparkly dress was with them. "I'm the Good Witch of the North. Welcome to the Land of Oz!" she said. She gestured to her companions. "My friends, the Munchkins, are very grateful to you for killing the Wicked Witch of the East. You have set them free at last."

Puzzled, Dorothy looked down and saw two legs wearing a pair of sparkly red shoes poking out from underneath her house. She gave a little scream and watched in horror as the legs shriveled away to nothing, leaving only the shoes.

"Who was she?" Dorothy asked the Good Witch.

"She was a very powerful, wicked witch," the Good Witch replied, taking in Dorothy's plaited pigtails and blue-and-white-checked dress. "You must be a great sorceress indeed, even if you do dress rather oddly." She noticed Dorothy's simple black shoes and gasped as if in pain. "Ugh! How hideous!" she said, and picked up the Wicked Witch's red slippers. "You'd better take these. They hold some kind of magical charm or other, but we don't know what it is."

Dorothy was surprised to find that the lovely slippers fit her perfectly. Thanking the Good Witch, she politely asked for directions back to Kansas, as she knew Aunt Em and Uncle Henry would be terribly worried about her.

"I've never heard of Kansas," said the Good Witch. "The Land of Oz is surrounded by a desert. It is impossible to leave."

Dorothy felt very sad and began to cry softly. Seeing this, many of the Munchkins pulled out their handkerchiefs and began to cry too. They sobbed giant wet tears and blew their noses with noisy honking sounds, which so amused Dorothy that she soon forgot her own tears.

"There is one thing you could try," said the Good Witch. "A powerful wizard lives in the Emerald City. He may know a way of getting you home."

"How can I find the Emerald City?" asked Dorothy.

"You must follow the yellow brick road to the center of Oz," she replied. "But beware! Don't stray from the road."

Dorothy was determined to find the wizard and get home as soon as possible. She thanked the Good Witch and the Munchkins and set off along the yellow brick road with Toto trotting along beside her.

After several miles, the yellow brick road passed through a cornfield. Beside the road was a scarecrow. As Dorothy and Toto passed by, he winked at them! Dorothy gasped and jumped back, and Toto got such a fright that he leaped into a prickly bush.

"You wouldn't mind lifting me down, would you?" the Scarecrow asked politely. "I don't weigh much."

Toto barked and growled at the Scarecrow as he plucked prickles out of his rump with his teeth, but Dorothy thought he seemed nice enough. He was certainly the nicest scarecrow she'd ever met.

Dorothy helped the Scarecrow down to the ground. He thanked her and asked where she was going. Dorothy explained that she was going to see the wizard.

The Scarecrow looked very excited. "May I come with you?" he asked. "Maybe the wizard could give me a brain." He lifted his hat and pulled a handful of straw from his head. "I so wish to be smart, but I only have straw for brains."

Dorothy was happy to have company and told the Scarecrow he may join her, and they set off along the yellow brick road together, chatting merrily.

Later that day, they came upon a woodcutter's cottage. Outside it stood a man completely made of tin who was holding an ax in mid-air, ready to chop at a tree branch. He seemed to be frozen in place.

"Would you be so kind as to oil my joints?" the Tin Man asked through his creaky, rusted jaw. Dorothy found an oilcan close by and oiled the Tin Man's joints until he could move freely. He was very grateful.

When Dorothy told the Tin Man where she was going, he asked if he could join them. "I've heard of the Great Wizard of Oz," he said, "and I'm sure he could give me a heart. I only want to love and be loved, but that's very hard without a heart." He banged on his tin chest with his tin fist, and it made a hollow, clanging sound.

Dorothy agreed that he should join them, and they set off along the yellow brick road once more.

The road led them through a dark and gloomy forest full of strange screeches and squawks and grunts and growls. Suddenly, a huge lion leaped out onto the road ahead of them and let out a ferocious roar. Toto barked and the Lion bared his teeth and tried to bite him!

"Don't you dare eat my dog!" Dorothy cried, stepping forward and smacking the Lion on the nose. "You should be ashamed of yourself, a big beast like you, trying to eat a little dog! You are just a big coward!"

The Lion's jaws snapped shut, his eyes welled up, and, to Dorothy's great surprise, he began to cry. "I've always been a coward," he said through his sobs. "I wish I was brave, but I just can't help being scared."

Dorothy felt very sorry for the poor creature and suggested that he join them on their journey. "I'm sure the wizard can give you some courage," she said. The overjoyed Lion promised he would not try to bite Toto again.

They traveled further into the forest and came to a wide river that had a rickety wooden bridge over it. Just as they were about to cross, the group heard terrifying sounds coming from the forest around them.

The Lion gasped in fright. "The Kalidahs!" he whispered. Several beasts stepped out of the trees and Dorothy saw what had terrified the Lion so. The Kalidahs were giant creatures with bodies like bears and heads like tigers. They had razor-sharp claws and long pointy fangs.

"Everyone get across the bridge!" yelled the Scarecrow.

"We'll never make it!" cried Dorothy.

"I'll hold them off," said the Lion and he turned to face the Kalidahs. He roared his most terrifying roar, stopping the startled Kalidahs in their tracks. When everyone had reached the far side of the river, the Lion sprang on to the bridge and ran as fast as he could.

The Kalidahs gave chase. The Lion reached the far side as they started to cross, and the Tin Man began to chop at the bridge. The Kalidahs were almost across as the Tin Man struck his final stroke. The bridge gave way with a huge crack and fell into the river, and washed some of the Kalidahs away.

Dorothy and her friends hugged each other with relief. Keen to get out of the dark forest, they had a short rest, then continued on their way.

The next morning, they reached the edge of the forest and were very excited to see a shining city in the distance. "That must be the Emerald City!" cried Dorothy, and she began to run along the road, the others close behind.

As they ran, Dorothy and her friends came upon a vast field of brilliant red flowers. Instead of following the road, which ran in a circle around the field, they took a shortcut through it. They plunged into the field, whooping and leaping and giggling as the flowers tickled their legs.

Little did they know that the flowers possessed a powerful magic. Dorothy soon slowed to a walk. A wave of weariness washed over her and she sat down. Within a few moments, she was fast asleep. Toto, too, slipped into a weary slumber, then the Lion suddenly stopped and dropped to the ground, fast asleep too.

The Scarecrow and the Tin Man were not made of flesh and blood, so they weren't affected by the magic. "Oh no!" the Scarecrow cried over the Lion's ear-splitting snores. "We must get them out!"

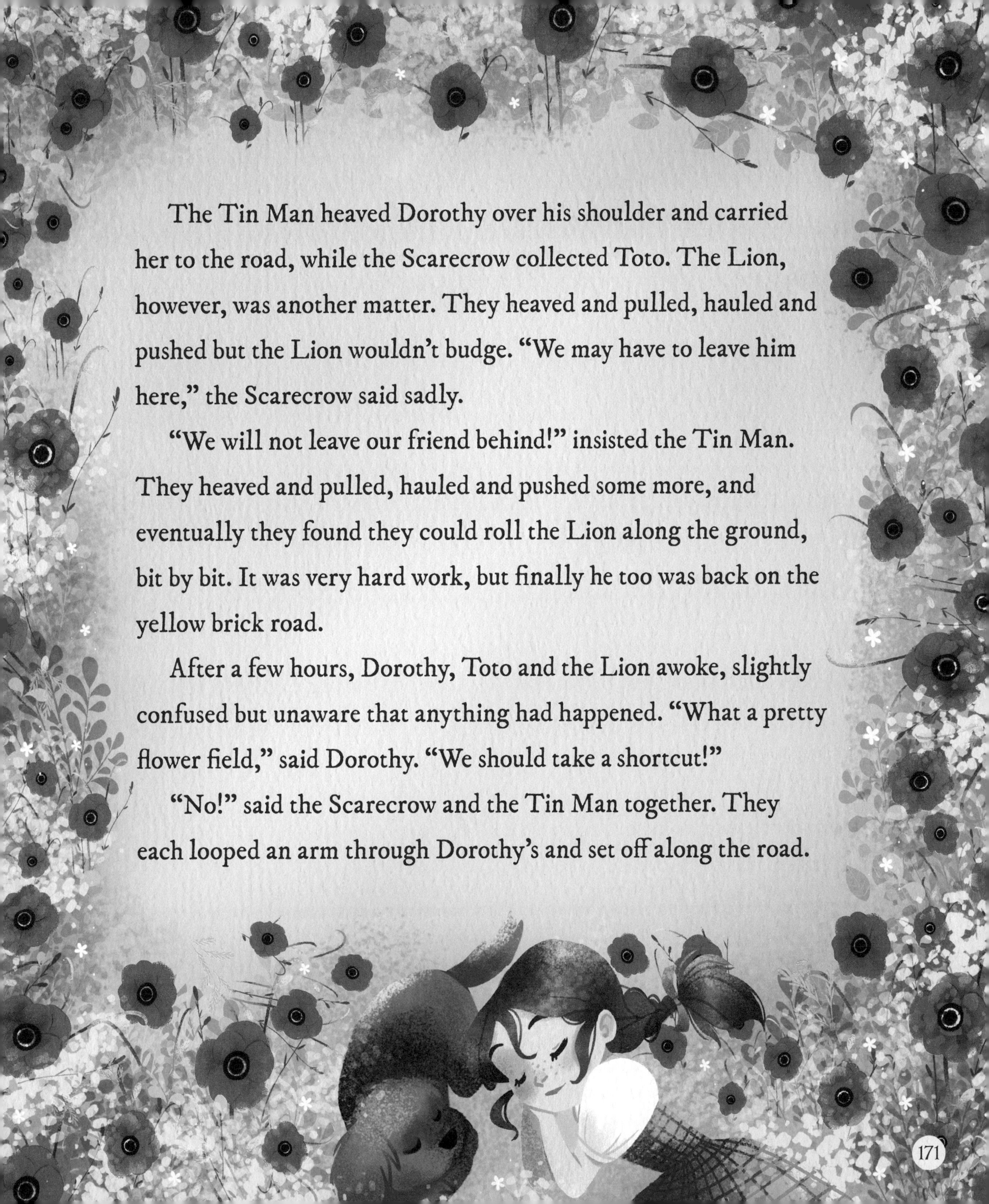

The Tin Man heaved Dorothy over his shoulder and carried her to the road, while the Scarecrow collected Toto. The Lion, however, was another matter. They heaved and pulled, hauled and pushed but the Lion wouldn't budge. "We may have to leave him here," the Scarecrow said sadly.

"We will not leave our friend behind!" insisted the Tin Man. They heaved and pulled, hauled and pushed some more, and eventually they found they could roll the Lion along the ground, bit by bit. It was very hard work, but finally he too was back on the yellow brick road.

After a few hours, Dorothy, Toto and the Lion awoke, slightly confused but unaware that anything had happened. "What a pretty flower field," said Dorothy. "We should take a shortcut!"

"No!" said the Scarecrow and the Tin Man together. They each looped an arm through Dorothy's and set off along the road.

Eventually they reached a huge green gate studded with glittering emeralds and surrounded by towering city walls made of green brick.

Dorothy banged three times on the gate. Soon a shutter opened and a man in a green hat poked his head out. "State your business," he said.

"We are here to see the Wizard of Oz," said Dorothy. The man opened the gate and escorted them to the palace. They were taken to a great room with a green marble floor and an emerald-colored curtain that covered an entire wall.

After waiting for what seemed like a very long time, a voice boomed through the room. "I am Oz, the Great and Terrible. Who are you?"

Dorothy was frightened, but found the courage to speak. "I am Dorothy, sir," she said. "A great wind carried me and my house to the land of Oz and now I am stranded here."

"Aha!" boomed the voice. "So you are the one who killed the Wicked Witch of the East?"

"I suppose I am," replied Dorothy, "but it really was an accident."

"And what do you want of me?" asked the voice.

Dorothy explained that she wished him to help her get home to Kansas. Then she introduced her friends and explained that they sought a brain, a heart, and some courage.

After a long pause, the voice replied, "I will grant all you ask, but first you must complete a task. You must travel to the castle of the Wicked Witch of the West and destroy her."

Dorothy burst into tears. "But I've never killed anyone or anything on purpose in my life. And even if I wanted to kill her, I don't have a spare house!"

"You'll think of something. Now go!" boomed the wizard.

The band of friends left the Emerald City and followed the yellow brick road to the strangely empty and quiet lands of the Wicked Witch of the West. They had no idea how they would destroy the Witch, or even if they would be able to find her.

They needn't have worried, however, as the Witch had already seen them from the tallest tower in her castle. Furious that they were trespassing on her land, she hopped up and down, muttering to herself and scratching at her warty face.

Then she took out a golden whistle and blew three long notes. Soon there was a great fluttering and an army of winged monkeys swarmed around her.

"Fetch me that wretched girl and the lion!" the Witch told the King of the Monkeys. "Destroy the others."

The winged monkeys nodded and flew away. They grabbed up the Lion and Dorothy, who clutched Toto close to her chest. Then they pulled the stuffing out of the Scarecrow so he was nothing more than a pile of rags and dropped the Tin Man from a great height so that he broke into pieces.

The monkeys took Dorothy and the Lion to the Wicked Witch. They held each other and trembled as the Witch rubbed her hands together and cackled. She was staring at Dorothy's shoes. "I've wanted those magical, oh-so-sparkly shoes for so long," she said, "and now they're finally mine!"

Then she looked at the Lion. "And you'll do a good job pulling my chariot when I go for a drive! Everyone in Oz will remark at my noble steed and my beautiful slippers!" she said, and she danced an odd little jig that flicked up her skirt, revealing a pair of hairy legs with knobbly knees.

Though terrified, Dorothy and the Lion could not help but chuckle. The Witch became very angry and lunged toward Dorothy. "Now give me those shoes!" she cried.

This made Dorothy most cross. She picked a nearby bucket of water that had been left on the floor and angrily splashed its contents over the Witch, who began to shriek.

"Noooo!" cried the Witch. "I'm melting!" And so she was. Soon all that was left of her was a sticky brown puddle.

"You did it!" cried the Lion, and he picked up Dorothy and spun her around. Even Toto was springing merrily into the air, splashing in the puddle and making happy little yaps.

Dorothy and the Lion returned to the forest to find their friends. They put the Tin Man back together and filled the Scarecrow with fresh straw. They were as good as new in no time at all.

The merry little band followed the road back to the Emerald City. The countryside, which had seemed eerie and deserted before, was now filled with people who were all rejoicing the death of the Wicked Witch of the West.

When they arrived back in the Emerald City, they were taken once again to the great room. After a long wait, the voice boomed out, "You have destroyed the Wicked Witch of the West!"

"Yes," replied Dorothy. "Now all we ask is that you give us the rewards you promised."

"Well," said the voice, "that may be somewhat difficult." As the voice spoke, Toto ran over to the curtain covering the back wall and began tugging at the corner. Soon the whole curtain fell away, and behind it was a little man with thick spectacles, which made his eyes appear very large.

Dorothy was shocked. "Why, you're not a wizard! You're just a man!" she exclaimed.

The man huffed and puffed as if about to argue, but finally came further into the room. "I'm sorry, dear," he sighed. "I arrived in Oz when my hot-air balloon drifted away from my homeland and landed here. The people thought I was a wizard, as I came from the sky. I was a little frightened, so I let them believe it."

"But why did you promise us help you couldn't give?" asked Dorothy, feeling very sad.

"I meant well," replied Oz. "I have grown to care for the people of this land very much. You did us all a great service by ridding us of the Wicked Witch."

"But what about my brain?" asked the Scarecrow.

"And my heart?" asked the Tin Man.

"And my courage?" asked the Lion.

Oz jumped up from his chair excitedly. "I believe I can help with those," he said and he ran off behind the curtain.

When Oz returned, he lifted off the Scarecrow's hat and filled his head with a handful of pins and needles. Then he sewed it up. "From now on, you shall certainly be sharp-witted!" said Oz.

The Scarecrow was delighted. "I feel so smart!" he said. "I'd tell you all the smart things I'm thinking, but only I'm clever enough to understand." Dorothy smiled. She thought the Scarecrow had been perfectly smart all along.

Oz went behind the curtain again and this time returned with a small satin heart filled with sawdust. He cut a small hole in the Tin Man's chest, placed in the heart, and repaired the hole. "Now you have a brand-new heart!" he said.

The Tin Man was overjoyed. He hugged everyone in the room and told them he loved them so very much. Dorothy giggled, thinking how kind-hearted the Tin Man had been since the day she met him.

Finally, Oz went behind the curtain and returned with a bottle of liquid, which he offered to the Lion. "Drink this and you'll be the bravest Lion in Oz," he said.

The Lion gulped down the liquid quickly, then pranced and prowled around the room, bellowing his most ferocious roar ever. Oz leaned over and winked at Dorothy. "It was only water in the bottle, but it seems to have helped him find his inner courage," he whispered. This made Dorothy giggle again. After their very first meeting, she'd always found the Lion to be very courageous indeed.

"Now, my dear," Oz said to Dorothy, "I have an idea that might just see us both home. We'll make another hot-air balloon and sail across the desert all the way to Kansas. My home is not far from there."

Over the next days and weeks, Oz, Dorothy, and her friends worked on the balloon until it was finally ready. Oz and Dorothy said a tearful goodbye to their friends and the townsfolk, then climbed into the basket. The balloon began to rise, but at the last moment, Toto leaped out of Dorothy's arms and ran off. Dorothy immediately jumped out to chase him.

The balloon lifted from the ground and began to strain against the ropes that held it down. "Hurry, my dear!" cried Oz. But finally–snap!–the ropes broke, and the balloon sailed away.

"Farewell!" cried Oz, waving as the balloon rose higher and higher. That was the last anyone ever heard of the Great Wizard of Oz, but he was always remembered fondly.

Poor Dorothy slumped to the floor and began to cry. She cried and cried until she heard a soft, friendly voice say, "No need for tears."

Dorothy looked up to see a kindly looking lady with rich red hair and bright blue eyes, wearing a beautiful white dress. "I am Glinda, the Good Witch of the South."

"Pleased to meet you," said Dorothy, hiccupping as she tried to control her sobs. "But you don't understand . . . now I will never get home."

"Oh, yes you will," said Glinda cheerfully. "Your shoes contain a very special type of magic. Just knock your heels together three times and ask to be carried to wherever you would like to go."

If she had known, Dorothy could have gone home any time she liked! But then she would never have had such a grand adventure and made so many wonderful friends.

Dorothy smiled and dried her tears. She hugged each of her friends tightly, then picked up Toto and tapped her heels together three times. "Home to Kansas!" she said.

Instantly, she and Toto went whirring through the air, so swiftly that all Dorothy could feel was the wind whistling past her ears. In no time at all, she felt a gentle bump as she landed on the ground again.

"Good gracious!" Dorothy cried as she looked around. She was back home at the little farm on the prairie. There was even a new house in place of the one the wind had blown away.

And there was Aunt Em rushing toward her. "Darling girl, wherever did you come from?" she asked as she folded Dorothy into her arms and covered her face with kisses.

"From the Land of Oz," said Dorothy gravely. "And I'm so glad to be at home again!"

THE END

NOTES FOR THE READER

PETER PAN

Created by Scottish author and playwright J. M. Barrie, the character of Peter Pan first appeared in a 1902 novel for adults called *The Little White Bird.* Barrie based Peter Pan and the Lost Boys on the five boys of the Llewelyn Davies family, whom he met while playing in Kensington Gardens. Many of the tales in *Peter Pan* came from the games they played with Barrie, who played the part of Captain Hook.

Barrie wrote the play *Peter Pan,* otherwise known as *The Boy Who Wouldn't Grow Up,* in 1904. It was very successful and was performed each year for the next decade. It was updated over the years; Barrie added fairy dust to make Peter fly, stating: "... I had to add something to the play at the request of parents ... about no one being able to fly until the fairy dust had been blown on him; so many children having gone home and tried it from their beds and needed surgical attention." The production featured a small house constructed on stage for Wendy, and playhouses are now commonly called "Wendy houses" in the United Kingdom.

Barrie released the novel based on the play, called *Peter and Wendy,* in 1911. It has been published in many versions, with several film adaptations made over the years, including an animated Disney movie. In 1929, Barrie gave the book's copyright to a London children's hospital, the Great Ormond Street Hospital.

ALICE IN WONDERLAND

Alice in Wonderland started as a story told on a rowboat. On July 4th, 1862, Charles Lutwidge Dodgson and Reverend Robinson Duckworth set off along the Isis River from Oxford with the three daughters of Henry Liddell (Vice-Chancellor of Oxford University), named Lorina, Alice, and Edith.

Alice asked Dodgson for a nonsense story, so he entertained them with an improvised tale featuring her. He jotted down the story the next day and added to it on further outings, before starting work on writing the book in earnest in November. It was finished in 1864 and given to Alice as a Christmas gift, complete with illustrations.

Friends encouraged Dodgson to publish it, but it wasn't until a six-year-old said he wished "there were 60,000 copies of it" that he submitted it, with new illustrations. It sold out almost immediately. Its sequel, *Through the Looking-Glass and What Alice Found There,* was released in 1871.

Dodgson first used the pen name "Lewis Carroll" when he published a poem in 1856. He based it on his given names: Charles (Carroll) and Lutwidge (changed to Lewis), with the order reversed.

Today, *Alice in Wonderland* is one of the best-known children's stories. It's been translated into hundreds of languages and published in many editions. There have been *Alice* movies, television programs, radio shows, operas, plays, musicals, songs, pantomimes, and even a ballet.

TREASURE ISLAND

Treasure Island first appeared as a serialized story in a children's magazine called *Young Folks*. Originally called *The Sea Cook: A Story for Boys,* it was written by Scottish author Robert Louis Stevenson between 1881 and 1882, and published as a complete book in 1883. The idea came from a map of an imaginary island drawn by Stevenson and his 12-year-old stepson one rainy day in 1881. Our modern view of pirates owes much to *Treasure Island*, including clichés such as peg-legs, parrots, and treasure maps marked with an "X."

Stevenson was a successful novelist who also wrote *Kidnapped* and *Strange Case of Dr. Jekyll and Mr. Hyde.* He was often ill with tuberculosis, but traveled widely and wrote many travel essays. His journeys included walking tours in Europe, and he is credited with commissioning the construction of one of the first sleeping bags for those trips. His failing health saw him moving between Scotland, England, Europe, and America, trying to find somewhere to recuperate.

Stevenson traveled the Pacific, visiting Hawaii, where he became friends with King Kalákaua, continuing on as far as New Zealand. He settled in Samoa, where he was named "Tusitala:" Samoan for "Teller of Tales." He was much-loved by the local people: when he died aged 44, the Samoans sat guard with his body through the night, then carried him to a mountaintop, where he was buried overlooking the sea.

THE WIND IN THE WILLOWS

Kenneth Grahame wrote *The Wind in the Willows* in 1908. The book wasn't well received by reviewers, but the public loved it, with the book being reprinted numerous times.

The book had some famous supporters. U.S. President Theodore Roosevelt wrote to Grahame, saying he'd "read it and reread it, and have come to accept the characters as old friends." It was the favorite book of *Winnie-the-Pooh* author A.A. Milne, who adapted part of the story into a musical called *Toad of Toad Hall* in 1929.

The Wind in the Willows started out as bedtime stories that Grahame told his four-year-old son. The stories continued and evolved in a series of letters that Grahame sent to his son when he was away. Grahame worked as the Secretary of the Bank of England and had stories published in the literary magazines of the day, some of which were successfully published in several collections.

When Grahame retired from his position at the bank in 1908, the family moved to the Thames Valley in Berkshire, where Grahame himself had grown up. There he took those bedtime stories and letters and expanded them into the manuscript for *The Wind in the Willows.* The book was initially published without illustrations, but many illustrated editions have been produced. Perhaps the most famous is the 1931 edition illustrated by E. H. Shepard, who also created the illustrations for the *Winnie-the-Pooh* stories.

BLACK BEAUTY

Black Beauty was written by Anna Sewell and published in 1877. It was written in a time when horses were the main form of transport, used for riding and for pulling carriages, wagons, plows, and even canal boats. Horses worked everywhere: in cities on cobbled roads, in coal mines, on farms, and in factories. Industry, farming, and society needed horses to function.

Anna Sewell wrote *Black Beauty* to highlight the terrible living conditions of many horses. Aged 57 when the book was published, she had spent most of her life relying on horses to get around due to a childhood injury. It's thought that the family's much-loved black horse Bess was the inspiration for Beauty.

Black Beauty was Anna's only book. It was enormously popular as soon as it was released and is one of the best-selling books of all time. Sadly, Anna Sewell died five months after the book was published, but she did live to see its success. By 1879, there were over a million copies sold in the United States.

One of the important legacies of *Black Beauty* is the awareness it brought to animal welfare. It was instrumental in the banning of the bearing rein, which painfully pulled a horse's head back and caused chest and lung problems, and helped build public interest in legislation to prevent animal cruelty.

THE WIZARD OF OZ

Written by L. Frank Baum, *The Wizard of Oz* was published in 1900. Before the book was published, Baum had been a poultry breeder, a playwright and actor, and a newspaper and journal editor.

In 1899, Baum's second book, a collection of nonsense poetry called *Father Goose, His Book,* became the best-selling children's book of 1899. Baum worked on that with the artist W. W. Denslow, who also illustrated *The Wizard of Oz.*

The original publisher of the book agreed to print *The Wizard of Oz* because it was also being made into a stage musical. The publisher and Baum shared the copyright of the book, but had a falling out over the royalties from the musical and never worked together again.

Baum supposedly got the name for Oz when, struggling for an idea, he looked around his study and saw his filing cabinet. The bottom drawer was labeled "O to Z." The book was a bestseller, and spawned thirteen sequels, plus twenty-one further books by Ruth Plumly Thompson after Baum died in 1919.

There have been musicals and film adaptations, including silent movies and the well-known 1939 film, *The Wizard of Oz.* That film changed several elements from the book, two elements of which are that a whole section at the end of the book was omitted from the film, and the film had Dorothy waking up to find it had all been a dream.

ILLUSTRATORS

LYN-HUI ONG
Peter Pan

AGNÈS ERNOULT
Alice in Wonderland

GEORGE ERMOS
Treasure Island

LEE HOLLAND
The Wind in the Willows

JAVIER SALAS &
PATRICIA MACCARTHY
Black Beauty

GERALDINE RODRIGUEZ
The Wizard of Oz